The Death of a Pilgrim.

By

A D Thorne

# DISCLAIMER

Disclaimer:

# COPYRIGHT

# CHAPTER ONE

## *The girl on the fence*

It was the first day of April, a Sunday, when Richard Harris opened his small art gallery for summer and looked round in satisfaction. The hard work of the winter to add fresh paint and modern chairs had been worthwhile because several new paintings now adorned the walls and created a homely atmosphere. Although it was still a showroom, with a cathedral ceiling and expanse of white wall, the cosy grey seating scattered with cosy and contrasting cushions gave a warm welcome to clients. When they felt comfortable, they stayed longer, chatting and often bought a painting.

He admired his work from the open doorway, whilst welcoming the early pilgrims of the spring. Not the first because 'The Camino de Santiago' never closes and some prefer the solitude in winter, but when the pilgrim hostels and bars shut down in autumn. There were fewer who passed his door.

Because he enjoyed the human contact, he always

struggled to decide whether to open during the wet weather. So instead, he opened at weekends and closed in January when the rain turned tracks to mud and icy cobbles deterred everyone but the most hardy. The extra time gave him a chance to refill the gallery walls and make his popular postcards and prints. Visitors told him they loved his ethereal, often delicate watercolours and he hoped that his faith added meaning and emotion, revealing glimpses of life.

During the previous year, a wooden screen had separated the showroom from the workshop. But in the busy summer months, he was self-conscious painting with strangers in the room and on one occasion a well-meaning pilgrim had worked on his canvas, thinking it was a public project.

So when he closed for the season, he cleared out a stable attached to his cottage. With the help of a local builder, he installed a concrete floor, windows, and a wood-burning stove, finishing a week before the inauguration and giving him a new private studio. He registered as a professional artist and today he paced back and forth, eager to greet customers.

The following day, long before it was light, he trudged up the hill for his breakfast. The restaurant stood in isolation, three kilometres from the nearest village and at the top of a steep climb, halfway between *Triacastela* and *Sarria*. Most summer mornings, he walked up for his early morning coffee. Today, through the dining-room window, the sea of mist dissolved into wispy columns over the valley, creating a view that made the effort worthwhile.

A bomb had shattered his right leg and hip years before and he needed regular exercise to keep mobile. The distance both ways served that purpose and if he arrived before seven, he could be back in his gallery by eight.

In the winter, when this bar was closed until lunchtime, he walked into the village with its shops, bars and restaurants, only fifteen minutes' walk away from home.

This morning he crumbled the croissant that came with the strong Spanish coffee with an odd sense of foreboding.

With a deep breath, he summoned the courage to hand over his new business cards as he was leaving. Then was relieved that Raúl attached them to the notice board. In his time as a police detective, he hadn't hesitated to introduce himself because his height and bearing offered a clue to his purpose before he spoke.

Now, stooped and thinner, his clothes hung from a sparse frame. He didn't recognise himself from those days. When he shaved, eyes lacking any assurance and sparkle gazed back from a pale crumpled face and his daily walk was more for fresh air and basic mobility than fitness.

Outside, the wind was frigid and with no trace of mist. A wisp of wood smoke, tractor diesel, the damp of a winter dawn, and the aroma of cow muck on the fields made up the familiar scents of morning.

He loved to stroll into the sunrise, with the sky still dark other than a pink glimmer on the horizon. The glorious display as the sun rose became his own personal inspiration, unique, and he never grew tired of the steady movement of colour across the landscape, bringing him home in time for his first customers.

He had tried to recreate the elusive dawn light on paper, but it was never right. It was God throwing a challenge.

*"Look, this is what I can do. What about you?"*

Several attempts were on his gallery wall and he

periodically caught a customer looking, head tilted to one side, lingering to see what the sun revealed.

Many of his paintings were of the Camino in various guises, winding through trees, in mountains, tucked in between snow-covered houses, maybe a glimpse of a pilgrim, sometimes only a ghost.

He stretched an old grey hat over red tipped ears as he meandered towards home. Occasionally, someone passed in the other direction, making him jump by shouting.

*"Hola. Buen Camino."*

In August, pilgrims crowded this path, outnumbering locals, and numbers rose every year. For the moment, he relished the quiet.

The pain in his leg confined itself to poor weather, and he had replaced heavy crutches for re-enforced walking poles, which drummed an irregular beat as he compensated for his damaged hip and pelvis. A morning walk energised him and, even with his injury, was a highlight of his day.

Lost in the gentle charm of Galicia, the forests and hills, the green fields and the tranquillity, he no longer thought he had made a mistake in coming. Sometimes he was lonely, but he didn't think London was better, simply busier.

Light was spreading across the sky, but the pinks and reds faded as he ambled toward home. Spain is a country where everything is late. So it was too early yet for the farmers, postal delivery officers, parents, or shopkeepers. Only foreigners and the bar staff who needed their business ventured out before daylight.

The morning was his, and as he increased his pace, he owned it. With the road to himself, his spirit lightened as shook off the foreboding he had woken with, eager now to open his gallery and greet today's guests. He suspected that when the season ended in October, the excitement might wane, but today his enthusiasm grew as he spotted his house through the trees.

There was someone leaning on the fence that divided the track from his garden.

When he saw them, he hurried as much as his sticks allowed, his limp becoming more and more pronounced. The gallery was chilly, but he had laid the fire ready for a match and planned to offer a coffee whilst they waited.

He couldn't determine the gender because clothes for walking appear unisex. When waving his hand and calling "*Hola*" elicited no reply, he called again.

"*Hola, Hola.* Hello,"

Many pilgrims spoke English. But he always greeted them in Spanish because he thought it more respectful. There was no response, and Richard's earlier sense of foreboding returned.

Something in the way she stood disturbed him. The young woman, her dark hair escaping in curls from around her hat, was tall and slight, but at six foot one, Richard towered over her. Her hand gripped the railing, and her rucksack supported her upright position. She was dead, her skin waxy and devoid of blood.

On closer inspection, he found that a metal fence post between the woman's back and her pack kept her erect, her bag supporting her head.

He swallowed the acid that rose to his throat, glad now that he hadn't eaten a big breakfast and stood still for a moment, shocked, no, horrified. He had seen ample bodies in his career, but not outside his home. On his second approach, he touched her neck to confirm his conclusion, scanning her body for the cause of her demise.

It took a minute to react and even when he realised he should phone for help; he wasn't sure that his language was fluent enough to explain.

"A girl is dead, a pilgrim."

"No, the police and an ambulance!"

He spoke in slow Spanish stating it was an emergency, there had been a death, then repeated himself so the operator understood the urgency.

Someone was approaching, and he realised he must keep the public from the scene, so unlocking his gallery, he grabbed the screen that had once divided the room, placed it across the track. Then scribbled a note requesting they wait inside in comfort. His action might allow the girl her dignity, but in his experience, the power of curiosity was strong. But then, he only needed a few minutes until the authorities arrived.

Waiting was not a euphemism for inactivity and without thinking he became a detective, so it was with a professional eye he analysed the scene, taking photos, making notes in the notebook he carried, noting a hole in her jacket, edged with blood, and querying why there wasn't more.

The sound of an approaching vehicle did not slow his observations. Once again, he scanned the young woman, noting that her gear was an expensive technical range and her backpack bigger than the ones most experienced hikers use. She must be strong and fit to carry it. It was easy to send unwanted equipment, by courier, to Santiago for collection on arrival.

A striking girl, he could see that, although the bulky hiking gear hid her features.

The undisturbed ground and the dirt track showed no

sign of a struggle. Someone had hung her on that fence. By the time he had noted the details, the ambulance was picking its way along the narrow approach to his gallery.

He took charge out of habit and stopped the paramedics before they reached her, preventing them from touching her and contaminating the scene. A tone of authority had crept into his voice and he stood taller.

A few minutes later, a police car pulled up, much to his relief, until he realised it was the local force who, in Spain, do not investigate serious crime. The ambulance crew and Richard reached the vehicle together and the young female officer opened the window and spoke to him in English.

"Señor Harris?"

"*Si,*"

"The office sent me because I speak your language. Can you explain the problem?"

"There has been an unexplained death." He tried to enunciate without falling back on British police shorthand. He pointed behind the vehicle, realising she could not see the girl from her seat.

"Have you confirmed the cause of death?" she said to the paramedic.

The ambulance driver looked at Richard and explained that they hadn't yet.

He intervened. "This may be a murder. It's important that we don't move the body."

"Our police force is excellent in Galicia so members of the public don't decide if someone has committed a crime."

She sounded indignant, as though he was implying they couldn't handle things. Now he realised his mistake. He was the civilian here and in his days as chief inspector, he would have seen it as interference.

"I'm sorry. Could you please come with me and I'll

show you?"

He opened the car door for her and waited. Both police officers climbed out and followed him round the ambulance without question.

The girl was there, still gripping the fence and staring along the blocked road. If it was possible, she looked more dead than when he had found her only fifteen minutes earlier. Her face was becoming a mask, less human, and both the police officers gasped. Ana, the one who spoke English, reached for her radio and called for the Guardia Civil to respond at once, explaining that it was urgent. The other was pale, verging on white, and leaned on the ambulance.

Ana asked for Richard's details after taking a notebook out.

"I need to see your identification first."

She communicated with care, articulating each word.

Richard reached for his bag and his ID and then remembered the pilgrims.

"My ID."

He offered her the folder of paperwork.

"But we have another problem. I diverted people from the scene into my showroom. They will grow impatient."

Then he walked along the lane, motioning for her to follow.

"This is my gallery, but my home is at the bottom of the steps." As the only Englishman in the neighbourhood, she must have known he was the English artist. Even strangers knew his house.

When they reached the door, she looked for her colleague, who was leaning against a tree, being sick and unable to help, so she entered the showroom alone while Richard waited by the exit.

Time slowed, and he checked his watch again. Only five minutes had passed and using his trekking poles to swipe at leaves stuck between the cobbles did not make it pass more swiftly. The frustration of a civilian when he itched to take control made waiting an agony.

The other officer had recovered and was chatting with the ambulance personnel. To Richard's relief, he had taken signs and created a no-go zone. The sign said 'Warning. Live animals,' which made him smile, but it showed initiative and it was a barrier.

He wanted another look at the girl, so he slipped through the gate, clambering over the flowerbed to the back of the girl's rucksack, grunting as he used his sticks on the steep slope.

The view from this angle confirmed why she remained upright. Her backpack was tall and sturdy, with a bulky hip belt, and the killer had placed the post between the pack and the girl. Her assailant had attached a hat to the frame, ensuring her head did not slump. Not a 'heat of the moment' response. Most murder scenes are messy, because it takes courage and callousness to move someone you have just killed and arrange them as flowers in a vase. This action needed planning, and a murderer with a reason to stage their crime. It was possible to walk past in the early morning light without realising that she was dead, giving the killer time to escape. But worse, he wondered if her assassin had placed her there for him to find, and it chilled him.

Maybe it was someone who knew his history, because although it sounded melodramatic for a countryside artist, for a police officer with a reputation for closing cases, and twice honoured for exceptional heroism, not so far-fetched and with a jolt he realised that the display might be for him.

After a few minutes in his garden where the sun was dispelling the mist that lingered along the stream, he walked to the road, mentally checking a list. There was no sign of struggle or trauma, nothing obvious left at the scene. When he studied the labels and the style of her equipment, he concluded she was English, young, and tall for a woman, five eight or nine.

Was she alone or part of a group? The conversations he overheard in his gallery suggested solo walkers formed fluid groups, so someone must know her, and others notice her she was an attractive woman.

Long ago, he and Gill had walked the Camino, and they were never lonely. He reflected on the friendships and a journey that changed him and his marriage. The sound of another vehicle approaching interrupted his memories.

The vehicle was a large 4x4 and after a moment, two officers in green military-style uniforms climbed out. An imposing man with an air of authority strode toward him.

# CHAPTER TWO

## *Guardia Civil*

The officer had a long, relaxed stride that covered the ground with ease and his expression of careless confidence suggested someone who enjoyed being in charge. The other officer went and chatted with the ambulance team and the local policeman who had recovered his composure and stood up straighter at her approach.

The detective greeted him, holding out his hand. "Miguel López. Are you Señor Harris?"

Richard's leg was painful and becoming hard to bend because he had been on his feet for three hours since leaving the café, so he found it hard to focus his attention on the man in front of him.

The officer spoke English with a London accent, somewhere central, and Richard raised his eyebrows in surprise

"My Galician parents brought me up in Hammersmith."

"I'm pleased you're here because someone murdered

her, do you want to take a look?"

As he pointed to the victim and moved towards her, the guardia frowned and opened his mouth to protest, but he spoke first.

"Former chief inspector, serious crimes, in the Met. I've seen my fair share."

He responded without turning, having mentioned his former occupation to save time. He expected hostility or surprise, but Miguel grinned like a schoolboy who had been offered a bag of sweets.

"Can't remember the last suspicious death, let alone murder here. Glad you're with us. Now show me the victim."

Richard's stick was clacking against the cobbled section of the road as the men walked toward the body together. He used the opportunity to study the detective because his limp slowed their progress.

They matched each other in height, but whilst he was pale with sandy hair reminiscent of his Scottish ancestry, Miguel was olive-skinned with black hair and eyes so dark you couldn't tell the iris from the pupil. The Spaniard was big and well-muscled. and with a boyish grin at odds with his build.

As they reached the fence, the doctor joined them, his car blocking the lane from the other direction. The guardia and the surgeon spoke before Miguel turned to Richard.

"Can you give me a summary of events before my friend here starts work?"

He was glad to articulate what happened and took care to include observations. Miguel (the officer, gave no sign of rank), handed him gloves.

"Pockets, rucksack and coat. Let's find out who she is."

So far his Spanish companion impressed him. The

detective wanted to see how he coped with searching the clothes of a corpse, testing his claim whilst maintaining a relationship that might prove useful.

There were only tissues and coins, so Miguel called his sergeant and the local police officer to take photos and then lift the deceased from the fence. After that, the doctor and the ambulance crew started the examination, removing the girl's pack and laying her on the track.

The young officer searched with commendable care, impressing him with her methodical approach. Meanwhile, the medical team was checking for further signs of injury with less assurance and no proper concern for preserving evidence. Maybe the surgeon, this far from a city, had no experience of murder.

While he was watching the medics, Miguel searched the scene and took photos of the surroundings. Every so often, the policeman asked the doctor a specific question, his eyes narrow as the physician carelessly handled the girl's body.

"Can we, at least, preserve the evidence?" the officer suggested, handing the scientist a pack of small bags.

The physician was oblivious. "I've finished now, and she is definitely dead, stabbed by the looks of it. I'm unsure of the autopsy procedure for murder, but I rang through for permission to move her."

"Don't worry, we'll keep her in the morgue and get an expert pathologist to assist you with the postmortem."

The doctor nodded.

Miguel was at ease with both crime scenes and inexperienced personnel, odd in such a remote place, and he wondered if the detective had worked somewhere else.

In the meantime, local officers were dealing with the crowd, who were becoming more curious and difficult.

Left alone, Richard was now without a role, a mere bystander.

The experience was emotionally draining, and he found himself in an unfamiliar position, a witness and a civilian, not able to use his knowledge and take control. Unsure that he liked the feeling, and in pain having overused his damaged leg, he slipped through the gate leading past his gallery. Then onto the steps beside his house to sit on a bench positioned in a sunny spot against his wall, swinging his legs around to lift the pressure off his damaged hip. At last, the sun dispelled the mist and warmed the thick granite behind him. He soaked up the sunshine after a long and wet winter. As he rested there, he smelled the spring, the grass, the emerging flowers in his garden and the river beyond that. The body hadn't developed the distinctive odour of death, but he imagined it because it was as much part of a murder site as blossoms in an orchard.

He wanted coffee and a chance to make notes, but his curiosity won and he remained outside, watching the work of the professionals.

Despite knowing that solving this case was someone else's responsibility, he posed the questions this job demanded and noted the answers in his notebook. This was a murder, and he watched the lane becoming a crime scene.

The most obvious suspect is the person who discovered the body and he wondered how he would cope with being questioned.

"We may have identified the girl. We found a passport and some papers."

Richard started and swung his legs back to the floor. He could hear a question in Miguel's statement:

"She's English?" he asked.

"Do you know her?"

"No, I don't think so." The comment had him wondering if there was something familiar in her features.

"But her walking equipment looked British. Can you tell me who she is?"

Discretion came with experience, especially when talking to a suspect, and Miguel hesitated.

"I'll give you the name in the passport. We haven't made a formal identification, so it is important that it remains confidential."

Richard nodded, knowing the score. The officer was watching his reaction.

"She is called Molly Hambleton."

To Richard's surprise, it sounded familiar but couldn't summon up a memory to explain the recognition.

"So, you recognise her?"

"I feel I should know that name, and that I've heard it before."

"She is not a family member or a friend…?"

He shook his head. "Look, I'm sorry. If I were you, I'd be suspicious at this stage."

Then, closing his eyes, he leaned back to reach for a memory he sensed but couldn't recover.

"The doctor suggested she was stabbed. Did he give you a time of death or any information about the weapon?"

"Yes. Is this your house, and do you have coffee?"

Richard nodded his affirmation, acknowledging that the officer wanted a private word. It took a moment to find the key, but once inside he saw Miguel glance round at the tidy, but chilly, open plan living room. Before making drinks, he lit the fire and then both men sat at the table, mugs warming their hands, and gazing as the flames edged around the logs.

"To be honest, this looks suspicious and I will need you to give a formal statement."

"No need to explain. Do you want me at the station?"

"No, not now," said Miguel. " But I require your ID, *residencia, empadronameinto,* NIE and passport, and your phone number so I can contact you."

Richard turned over the documents to him, the paperwork so readily available because Spain is bureaucratic and he needed it often.

"We would like to use your gallery whilst this remains a crime location. Do you have somewhere else to work?"

The tone was friendly, but it was a command.

He handed over the keys.

"My studio is in the old stable."

"Thank you, and we will respect your property."

"Until tomorrow." Miguel rose, offering Richard his hand. So he stood, using the chair, but then let the detective go without comment. His ID taken, and the crime scene outside his gate, confined him to his house. The man accomplished it while maintaining that he was a colleague and he admired that skill.

He had disliked dealing with the public, and his lack of conversational skills had made his wife wince. At work, his inspectors realised that bystanders, relatives and potential witnesses were their responsibility. They hadn't minded because Richard had been a superb interviewer, observant, and a good listener. Comfortable with silence, which most people can't handle. Suspects gave themselves away by being desperate to speak and fill the gaps in conversation. He would be a skilful poker player if he gambled.

The sun, setting behind the edge of the valley had tinged

everything with orange, giving his garden a sinister hue. With his eyes closed, he considered the day's events.

The pain in Richard's leg kept him seated, reminding him again that he was not the man he once was.

Miguel puzzled him, treating the scene as an expert, while claiming there were no murders here.

'So where did the officer learn how to act at crime scenes?' Not in Sarria, he concluded.

'What isn't he saying?' Richard wondered. The guardia hadn't offered his rank, and he was unfamiliar with the insignia that they used on their uniforms.

The sergeant was in awe of him, so she wasn't his regular 'bag-man', suggesting he might not be based locally. However, most high-ranking police officers are power hungry and competitive and even though he had sensed none of that in Miguel there was something... At a guess he had a higher rank than their equivalent to chief inspector from the reaction to his old status.

He was too important to visit a crime scene in a backwater such as Sarria. So what was he doing responding to a routine call out? Of course, it might not be normal in the countryside. London was always different.

Now he had recovered from the shock. He wished he had asked more questions.

This morning, with a stock of saleable work and his painful history behind him, he was confident he was starting again as an artist. Instead, here he was, caught like a lobster in a trap whilst his past reappeared as a ghost ship hidden in the mist.

He wondered if his new career as an artist was in tatters. Unsure of what he wanted now, he realised how much he had lost in giving up his old career.

# CHAPTER THREE

## *Colonel Miguel Lopez*

Miguel left after three hours, humming a song he had heard on the car radio earlier. The local policeman guarding the site saluted as his car bumped along the narrow lane from Richard's house.

"So the British artist used to be a detective," he said to sergeant Elvira Núñez-Gómez.

"We should be grateful he was, Sir, because he preserved the crime scene for us."

"True, we also need to thank the young local officer for translating. I wonder if she could act as an interpreter for this matter."

"Would you like me to contact the commander and enquire?"

He nodded, even though it wasn't his concern. Now that he had established murder, it was up to the garrison commander.

The young sergeant had been nervous when Miguel announced he planned to visit the scene. But once there, her initiative and quick thinking had impressed him enough to make a note about talking to her boss.

It was an unusual start to the week because only twice in the past year had anyone called them out this far. Once to locate and stop a reckless driver and once to move stranded cars in a snowstorm.

The drive to the garrison was quiet. The sun was at its highest and the car was hot and Sergeant Gomez cracked the windows open. And he gazed out, enjoying the Galician spring air with its faint scent of blossom. Madrid, where seasons pass so quickly, is different, and it made his appreciation even greater.

He had an office in the local garrison, meaning that he could extend his leave by working remotely. Now, after his recent promotion, his work was based in the city and meant leaving his family home near Sarria. His household must move to the capital, or he faced living alone in a flat away from his wife and children.

"Are you going to stay and handle the incident, sir?" The words broke through his revery.

"I'll talk to my team," said Miguel, without removing his eyes from the blossom filled trees that always edged the fields here.

A complication, challenging enough to delay his return to Madrid, would be welcome news, and he wondered, again, if accepting his promotion was the wrong thing to do.

It involved uprooting his entire family, losing the support of grandparents, and forcing his wife, Carolina, to rethink her career by giving up her job as a lawyer.

He loved his duty, with its complexity and politics. The adrenaline buzz that came with solving the worst international crimes was his motivation. Even though his world at work was dark, he enjoyed pitting his wits against clever, well-funded organisations and winning. Beside that, he was ambitious, proud to be the youngest person to hold the rank of colonel. His family meant everything, and he admitted Carolina saved him from himself.

Once in the barracks, he and the police officer separated. She carried a box of collected evidence and documents to check-in, and he went to his small and cluttered room to phone both his wife and his boss.

Sergeant Elvira knocked on his door as he was dialling his Madrid office.

"Sir, you'll want to hear this before you do that. I just did a quick computer search on our victim, and she is the daughter of a prominent British politician. Doesn't that mean that we call in your unit, anyway?"

"Sergeant, you have made my day."

Of course, it was inappropriate to be so gleeful when presented with a homicide with political implications, but the opportunity to ask for his team's help and spend an extra month in Galicia caused his heart to leap.

"Just don't forget we have nothing official until we finish the autopsy," she said.

He liked her confidence, but when he winked at her, she blushed a deep red and got flustered.

Next, he looked into Richard Harris, starting with contacts in London before requesting his service history.

While he waited for people to return calls, he phoned the bar where the Englishman had his morning coffee, checking his alibi, collecting information to confirm that Richard didn't have time to commit a murder.

Later, someone would check the hour of death against his statement and walk that stretch of the Camino.

The English artist was the most obvious suspect, but he liked the man, and he had already been useful. So he carried out his own analysis before the official one, to assess the likelihood of the Englishman's involvement.

Miguel spent the next hour on the phone, ensuring his team was on the way. To his surprise, the general, his boss, suggested he invite Harris to help with the investigation, dismissing fears of him being a suspect.

"If he's there, you won't lose him and the victim is English, so the Metropolitan police will be involved and an insider might prove useful. Have you checked his record?"

"Yes, sir, he has an interesting history with a reputation for clearing crime. Also, they rewarded him for bravery twice. The death of his wife might be why he opted for an early pension rather than a desk job."

"It sounds impressive. My opinion is that he's better involved than interfering."

There were things he didn't mention. Richard had risen through the ranks slowly because he was not popular with management.

The strange thing, according to Miguel's friend in London, was that Richard disappeared after his injury. There was no forwarding address, and he contacted no one, pissing off 'the powers that be' who had lined up media appearances to publicise his medal and raise the Met's profile. The Englishman was no politician then, either inside or outside the job.

Later, after a quick lunch, he phoned and told his wife that he would be home for another month, which pleased them both.

And, he was still sitting at his desk smirking when sergeant Elvira reappeared with a photo in her hand.

"Complication, sir". Elvira handed him the print: it

was the front page of one of Britain's tabloid newspapers. The headline was, 'He will always be my hero.' Underneath was a snapshot of Richard, his arm around Molly Hambleton, their victim, who was gazing at him. Both were in evening dress.

"Shit!" said Miguel.

# CHAPTER FOUR

## *Where do I fit in?*

It was now lunchtime, but Richard wasn't hungry because his stomach was reacting to a strange mixture of adrenaline, anxiety, and grief.

He had never experienced a week which started this way, despite his familiarity with murder.

It was surreal, but he felt alive despite the tragedy.

He washed the coffee cups whilst watching a paper suited policewoman fingerprinting his fence and wondered what he should do to occupy his time. First, he sat for a while on his patio, which helped him to collect his thoughts, but the weather wasn't pleasant enough to sit outside for long. So he tried his studio, which was sparse and tidy, illuminated by a skylight and a small window.

The white painted walls highlighted the natural stone round the door, and a pale ceramic floor tile made the place appear bigger and lighter than it was. A bench and a rack of finished pieces furnished the room, while wire shelves lined one wall full of materials and drying work. It did not inspire him. Too much else was happening, but he needed to continue, so as always, he took out his utensils, laying them on the table in front of him, brushes arranged by size and paints grouped into colours. Then he picked up a clean palette and a jar for water. A wide wooden shelf above the sink held palettes and jars opposite a collection of framed watercolours, and in the middle stood a large and elegant easel, the last gift from his wife.

The wrapping had remained untouched until last week because he thought it might cause him too much pain to use. But today he found the gleam of oiled wood and the warm satiny touch added to his sense of anticipation, and he remembered her encouragement and her belief in him.

Whenever he started painting, his custom remained the same, akin to a yoga mantra, until it calmed and focused his mind. When he finished, he had a routine, ensuring he put everything away piece by piece as he washed it. The room was clean, and he didn't understand the cluttered chaos that was stereotypically part of creativity.

So, he tacked his sketch to the board and was ready. A lone pilgrim in the distance on the winding Camino, encircled by pines, blue grey in the early morning light. The treetops, tinged by the first pink of the rising sun called 'The Way', was to be a centrepiece for his gallery, not a composition for sale.

The events so far today left him uncertain of his ability to create anything because he was already working the case in his imagination.

So he turned on his favourite music and glanced around the room, satisfied that he had organised his equipment in the manner he liked. At that moment, his focus returned, blocking everything but the work before him. He always performed this routine, and it was the familiarity that enabled him to concentrate. The more awful and complicated the case, the more detailed the composition became. And, as he painted the tiny details, his mind freed itself of debris and he remembered the links he wanted to make.

In London, he maintained this section of his life as separate and private. His team at the office hadn't known that he had paintings stored in large art folders. He kept them, but he worked to sell now, and it was different. When he sketched, his anxieties and feelings ended up on the canvas. A part of his soul was with the pilgrim that his painting depicted walking into the sunrise.

He didn't sleep well that night, although his body felt heavy and his eyelids drooped before he went to bed. But he dreamed of the girl on his fence, the dark hair curling around the edge of her hat over her white skin. In his dream, she talked to him.

"Where were you?" she said. "You didn't save me this time, did you?"

He looked at her in confusion, because his wife peered through the dead girl's eyes, saying,

"Where were you, Richard? You saved the others, but why didn't you save me?"

Disturbed, he got up and walked around, but it started again when he returned.

Better to give up and get dressed. Although when he opened his shutters, the window showed nothing but more darkness, no stars and not a hint of dawn. He made coffee and relit his fire without cleaning it, wishing he could take his daily walk to the bar for breakfast.

When Miguel took his documentation, he was effectively under house arrest. If he left, he imagined someone had been ordered to stop him and he had no intention of finding out.

The interior of his cottage was tiny, with only a bedroom, bathroom, and living kitchen. A covered patio with his studio and a small storeroom lay beyond it. Just enough space, with his garden and the gallery for spreading out. He wasn't used to spending his time indoors because keeping active kept the nightmares at bay and fended off his loneliness. So he painted until the afternoon and then, driven by hunger, adrenaline, and curiosity, he packed everything away and made himself lunch.

He could hear the mumble of voices above him and tried to guess what was happening, wishing Miguel would phone him, but realised it took time to confirm the ID and check out Richard's story and record first.

As he paced, he racked his brains, trying to remember where he had heard the girl's name before, occasionally stopping and shaking his head in frustration. Molly Hambleton, Molly Hambleton.

He had retired, so he was no longer a police officer. Until yesterday, he hadn't missed it for a moment. Now, he wished he knew what they were doing, knowing how important the early stages were. He took up a tray of coffee and biscuits to the team, a British thing to do. In Spain, workers take a break in a café or bar.

The officers gathered round, recognising it as a gesture of friendliness, stopping work for a time to chat. Although they shared nothing of importance, his eyes scanned the gallery, noting the familiar boards and tables. The routine reassured him it was so familiar. There were four officers there, none of whom he recognised. Two were setting up and others searching the garden and lane. Items were on the table, bagged, tagged, and noted. He couldn't stand there and watch, and his Spanish wasn't good enough for idle chatter, which they wouldn't welcome. So he left the tray and returned downstairs. Not wanting to venture into the patio in case the search restarted, he paced his kitchen.

Impatience hadn't been his problem when he was on the job. He was methodical in searching for evidence, quiet, taking time to think, so his patience and reticence to cut corners marked him out.

When Miguel arrived, he appeared dishevelled and Richard suspected he hadn't been to bed, although he had changed out of his uniform. Instead, he wore a black leather flying jacket over a sweater and his trousers looked to be the same ones. The man didn't look as imposing as he had, so he opened his fridge and offered him a beer. The officer hesitated only for a second before taking it.

"Here are your documents. You will need to give a formal statement later, but for now, the general, my boss, has invited you to join the investigation."

He sat opposite, holding his own bottle. "Have you checked my record?"

Miguel just nodded, but made no comment and Richard wondered if he might mention his medal, his injury, or the media coverage of the terrorist attack that cost his spouse her life, and him his health and career. To his relief, his new friend kept quiet, so he could keep those memories to himself.

"If I can help, I will," he said.

Miguel grinned. "Amigo. There is much to discuss. But first, I must see my wife, so she knows I'm still alive. An officer is coming to take your statement, so please include every detail in your account. I'll come back this evening and I hope by then that I'm able to confirm the girl's identity."

The Spanish police rely on fingerprints and DNA for identification. They didn't need her companions to name her, so the case could move forward even though her friends had not been located.

Miguel warned him not to miss the details for a reason. He turned it over in his mind, wondering if earlier he didn't mention something significant.

He bustled round his compact kitchen cleaning the already clean table, thinking as he worked. Then pouring himself another beer and getting out crackers and cheese, relieved that he was no longer confined to the house and delighted with the offer to join the investigation.

Over his snack, he noted his observations in preparation for Miguel's return and thought about his statement. The victim's name was familiar, so he pulled out his computer and found lots of results, suggesting she was famous. He continued scrolling, then slapped his head as the memory came back to him.

The daughter of Sir Giles Hardcastle, of course, she used her mother's surname. Sir Giles hosted the dinner at the exhibition and he recalled meeting them both. He knew her and didn't remember. She and her father were among the memories he had tried so hard to forget, to put those experiences behind him.

There was still a mystery surrounding Miguel. The way he described a superior suggested the cohesion of the unit is more important than rank. There was a special unit of judicial police who investigated international crime. He might belong to that.

The local policewoman, who had responded to his call, arrived with a detective to take his statement. She introduced herself as Ana and explained they had co-opted her as an interpreter. With a huge smile and effusive hand movements, she explained this opportunity was rare.

"There will be a need to interpret. Someone must inform the girl's relatives and I can help with that, and the British police might call for my interpretation. Colonel López could translate, of course, but his involvement with the investigation gives him many more important duties."

The guardia officer looked at her and spoke with a tone that caused her to blush.

*Colonel López,* that was why he was being cagey he was too high a rank to attend incidents. Why was someone so senior there?

Having given his statement, he returned to his studio, where the approaching dusk had put everything in deep shadow. Art had always been his relaxation, but here it had become his livelihood. Although the forensic team occupied his gallery, he needed to keep painting. The composition he was working on was symbolic of his life. Once he had organised the room, he got out his paints. The smell of paint mingled with the stove's smokiness drew him in, and the work enfolded him, as he concentrated on getting dawn light onto the canvas.

# CHAPTER FIVE

## *Tom and Sally are found*

Miguel stepped round the studio door after 8 o'clock, making Richard jump. It was rare that anyone disturbed him there, especially when it was getting dark.

"Are you ready? Let me take you to my office because there is worrying news and this case may become complicated."

Richard wiped his hands on a rag.

"Give me a minute." He responded as much to Miguel's expression as his words.

Less than an hour later, they were sitting at the colonel's desk, which smelled of dust and cleaning fluid. Papers filled every surface of the mismatched battered furniture, and ego and status didn't intrude into the room's appeal.

"This is from the coroner confirming the girl is Molly Hambleton. The murder weapon was a long narrow blade which pierced the heart. Unfortunately, she was still alive when the killer hung her on your fence and the reason there was little blood visible is that she bled into her stomach and chest cavity."

He frowned at the callousness of the act but waited, expecting more.

"The previous night she stayed in an albergue in Triacastela and was with a party of four pilgrims, one of whom may have been her boyfriend."

"Have you found them?"

"No, but we're looking and have statements from the hostel and the restaurant where they ate their meal."

He knew he had not yet heard the news that caused concern.

Miguel removed a photo from his drawer and handed it to him. It depicted him in evening dress with his arm around Molly Hambleton.

"Why didn't you tell me about it?" he said, handing him a second photograph, which included Sir Giles.

"You know her."It was a statement and not a question.

"I've met her. I came here to forget. Not her, but the whole thing."

"In this image, you appear to be close and we found it on her phone."

He picked up the other image and rubbed the thick paper between his fingers as his mind drifted back to that night.

"They took it at the medal ceremony. There were several people photographed with me for the press release," he said.

He kept his voice flat and felt the blood drain from his face, which he hoped was devoid of expression. Miguel by now must have researched his history, so he didn't offer details of the award.

"Is that the only occasion you met?"

"No. Before that, she came to the hospital with her father after my injury."

He remembered the pain from that time.

"That morning, they told me that my wife had died. Then before lunch, the doctor explained I needed another surgery, but the damage to my hip may not be repairable."

He paused and leaned back, trying to control his emotions.

"Later on, in the early afternoon, Sir Giles and Molly arrived complete with make-up artist and camera crew for a photo shoot. The photographer asked her to hug me and her father to shake my hand."

He remembered his fury and could still feel the heat of it.

"I called the nurse and demanded that they withdraw. But they didn't go. They thought I was joking, and that I craved the publicity. They kept telling me I was a hero, and I deserved recognition."

"Why did they want the photos?" asked Miguel.

"Mmm. " Richard wiped his damp palms on his trousers and tried to recover his composure.

"Both were at the bombing."

"Then what happened?"

"The doctor told them I was too sick to take part."

"You didn't like Sir Giles?"

"Giles Hardcastle is an MP; a junior minister, oily and self-serving. I met too many of his type, the breed who use people and then discard them, and who believe everything is an opportunity for making money or building ego."

"Tell me about the bombing. Where did it happen?"

The room faded as Richard cast his mind back to London, his thoughts full of emotion and memories.

"The museum held a public exhibition depicting the

history of the Houses of Parliament. Afterwards, they had arranged a private dinner hosted by Sir Giles Hardcastle and attended by MPs and parliamentary lobbyists. The speaker was a historian called Gregory Bonham." he said at last.

"You were on duty, protecting them?"

"It was my day off, and I was with my wife. Gill wanted to see the exhibition. A party of schoolchildren was ahead of us when I saw two men and acted on my instincts. I was told that they stabbed Gill as they tried to escape."

"You cleared the area and disarmed the explosive. But the detonator exploded, shattering your leg. I read the report."

"I remember nothing after entering the exhibition. Someone informed me later that I neutralised the device, but I still had the detonator on a chair beside me. There shouldn't have been an explosion." Richard's voice was bitter.

"The maker made a mistake, and Gill, my Gill."

He couldn't continue.

"I'm sorry to press you, but can we connect it to the murder here?" There was compassion in Miguel's eyes, but the set of his shoulders reminded Richard this was a police enquiry, not a friendly chat.

He paused and focused on the photographs again.

"Something convinced the minister that the terrorists meant the blast for him, hence the desire for press photos. But why kill his daughter and why now?" said Richard, pulling himself together with effort.

"But you never believed they intended the bomb for Hardcastle?"

"At the time I was beyond caring, but no..., no, I never

accepted it."

"And the terrorists?"

"Tried and convicted, but gave no reasons."

There was a knock on the door.

"We've found two of the people walking with the victim, sir. They're being brought in."

"I understood it was a group of four." Richard spoke automatically.

"Let me know when they arrive," said Miguel, dismissing the officer.

"Why not wait for the interviews and stay with my wife and me? It's not far, and you'd be welcome."

He was too tired and his emotions too raw to be sociable, but he didn't want to miss the interviews. You can never run away because your past will follow you wherever you go.


The evening was creeping into night, when Tom Miller and Sally James arrived. So Miguel greeted them and chatted over a coffee, saving the interview for the morning. He recorded the conversation. The young couple had left Molly and her boyfriend, Jack, eating breakfast in Triacastela because they asked to be alone, so the party arranged a rendezvous three days later.

Molly's death had upset them and Jack's absence worried them.

"We met a lot of friendly people, and there were one or two that caught our attention. This guy, we were sure, fancied Molly. A woman in a green coat. A couple who always wanted to join our group for dinner. The weird man with the dog. None of them hurt us, though," added Sally.

At that point, he did nothing more until morning and

arranged for them to stay in the barracks, taking their passports and asking them not to leave, and Richard smiled at that. The guardia are military and armed.

Miguel did not live on site, although he stayed overnight when he was working. There was available living space, as in the past serving officers occupied staff housing, but most now lived in the town in their own flat.

He and Caroline had moved into the family home, a fifteen-minute drive into another world, a farm in the river valley. There were two houses and a barn forming three sides of a square courtyard. The dark obscured any detail, but the sense of tranquillity was palpable. The kitchen that they entered appeared unchanged in the last hundred years, but a closer inspection revealed modern plumbing and lighting, new cupboards built to match earlier ones, and a gas cooker for use when the wood-fired range was not lit. Carolina greeted them in the well used and warm room.

"And the children?" asked Miguel.

"In their beds. They already ate their dinner. Let's sit by the fire in the *salón* and talk whilst we eat." She spoke in English the whole family were bi-lingual.

Carolina's wide smile and the way she hugged Richard and welcomed him to their home as if he were an old friend encouraged him.

"There's an apartment at the barracks to use whenever I am working late, but Carolina wanted to meet you, and she is irresistible."

"Can I ask why you are in Sarria, because surely someone with the rank of colonel works from a city desk? And your office is so..."

"Untidy?" said his hostess.

"Homely," responded Richard.

"Oh, I have a department in Madrid, but we are an operational unit who move to the incident. Until now I have persuaded people I should keep a room here. The arrangement has helped us all. Sarria, because it raises their profile. The commanding officer, because it keeps me on the team. Carolina lived in the city, but when the children came, they were happier here. Her practice is in town, and her parents and mine are close by. Now everything will change again."

"Why must they?" inquired Richard.

"Because of my promotion to colonel, a rank that gives me command of the entire unit, not just the operational team. The job is based in Madrid, which means the family needs to move."

"Do you feel divided between career and home?".

"I am addicted to both." Miguel kept his voice light, but the truth was evident.

"Is it confidential or can I join you?" said Carolina, as they settled in the comfortable *salón* of the farmhouse.

The look between them lingered and was so full of love that Richard's heart missed a beat as they reminded him of what he had lost.

Suddenly, aware of his loneliness, he hoped these people would become friends.

"Sit with us. There are no secrets at the moment.

The tone suggested Miguel was more worried about this case than normal and wondered why.

"Do you think this is political?" she asked, familiar with her husband's moods.

"There are many elements. The potential links to the terrorist incident that involved you concern me." he nodded in Richard's direction. "The homicide of a foreign

MP's daughter makes it an international event. So I have called in my team."

"A murder on the *Camino Francés* is grim news for Galicia. Will you involve the *Xunta? (regional government)*" asked Carolina.

Miguel turned to him to explain.

"The homicide of a pilgrim affects us in many ways. This case is a political hot potato and we must handle it with care. The Camino de Santiago is our primary source of tourism and a centre for our spirituality."

Carolina's confusion over what a hot potato was doing in a murder inquiry eased the tension.

"The boyfriend is missing. Perhaps it is a simple domestic incident," said Richard. "But then, I doubt you would involve yourself if that was the case."

He had been seeking to lighten the mood by offering a simpler explanation, as the serious conversation overshadowed Carolina's generous hospitality

For a moment, he regretted the circumstances that brought him here. He wished he was free to enjoy the lovely room, his glass of wine, the fire and the company and it must have shown on his face because Carolina said;

"Oh, Miguel's cases are never ordinary or straightforward. The only advantage of his promotion is it will tie him to a desk in Spain and he won't be getting shot at abroad."

Richard noticed the slight emphasis on the only.

"I admit, when I am here, it's me who wants to shoot people."

Miguel adopted a despondent pose, putting his head in his hands. Carolina threw a cushion at him, but he heard the truth in the words.

"Tomorrow will be an arduous day. Let's enjoy our

drink and the company for an hour before we sleep."

"This wine is too good to waste," said Richard, swirling his glass.

"Oh, this is my father's home-made. Let me open a bottle of my favourite local Mencia," and Miguel left to get a bottle.

With that, he sank back into his chair, enjoying himself. He hadn't been this happy since Gill died, and yet he was aware of a shadow of unease.

# CHAPTER SIX

## *Getting Involved*

The next day promised to be difficult, so they were out of the house before the children awoke, despite the late hour they had retired to bed. Miguel instigated a search for Molly's boyfriend on arrival, and they headed straight to the interview room where the duty sergeant brought in Tom Miller, and he was clearly upset.

"How long have you known Ms Hambleton?"

"Since we started university together, so about five years."

"And Jack, when did you meet him?"

"A few weeks ago, when we planned the trip. Molly rang to say she wanted her new boyfriend to come. As she lives in London in one of her dad's flats and we still live in Sheffield, we didn't know him at all. They visited us to plan the last details ten days before we flew, and that was the first time we met."

"Can we review the events of yesterday? In fact, perhaps you could start with the previous evening and tell me what happened in your own words."

He nodded and paused, his brows furrowed.

"We arrived in Triacastela at about three o'clock and booked into our hostel. Then we have a routine: finding our beds, a shower and sorting out any washing, followed by time to ourselves till supper. I sat in the albergue garden reading until six thirty, when we met to find a bar for a drink. There was an atmosphere that evening."

"And then?"

"Everyone relaxed after a couple of beers, but it wasn't the best of evenings. Sal and I did the talking. During our meal, Molly was silent and Jack was snapping, putting everyone down even more than usual, so we retired to bed straight after dinner. The next morning, the mood was better. After we packed and found a café for breakfast, Molly told us they needed space alone. Sally must have talked to her earlier, because she hustled me out of the café before I could say a word and insisted that we did the first five kilometres at twice our typical speed and we never saw them again."

"But you didn't take to Jack?"

Tom looked thoughtful. "Normally, you get to learn about someone on a trail spending so much time together, but I don't feel that I know him at all. Most of the time, he was arrogant and superior, treating us like kids. In the evenings, he always had plenty of money whereas we were keeping a strict budget, but I learnt nothing about his job or his family. Once he claimed he worked in finance but was not more specific. When I asked about his parents, he said 'oh the normal' and then changed the subject ... I suppose I didn't relate to him. No."

Sally supplied more information about Molly's relationship with Jack. Molly had told her the couple needed to spend time alone to work out the little niggles they were having.

"What did the couple argue about?"

"Molly learnt something about him, but I'm not sure what. I know they had some issues and wanted to deal with them in private."

"How close were you at university?"

"Oh, very. We had rooms in the same corridor in the hall and then lived in a shared house. I missed her when she moved to London."

"Did she have secrets? Was she involved with drugs or anything?" asked Miguel.

"No drugs. She didn't smoke or drink, but she had some dodgy friends and joined demonstrations and stuff."

"Dodgy in what way?"

"Hard to say. I didn't appreciate their sense of humour, so I kept away. Some were the children of politicians and aristocracy, they made jokes about students from comprehensive schools like me. Called themselves The Upper Crust or just UC. I saw them on a march demonstrating with some skinheads, protesting about immigration along with an organisation named 'First Nation' or 'One Nation' or something. The National Front were there as well."

"So nationalists or fascists?"

Maybe. Most of us were interested in injustice and protested. She was the only person I recognised with that group, and I don't think she kept in touch with them."

Neither knew where Jack might have gone. Nor did they know his address or phone number, as they used Molly as the contact. But they both offered their phones so that the technician could copy the relevant photos.

Something obstructed the images of him. In fact, there

wasn't one unobstructed shot. There were partial shots in which he appeared unaware of the camera, and Miguel hoped they could produce a composite photo. That might take days, so he asked Tom and Sally to stay in Sarria.

He doubted they were involved, but it was too early to rule anyone out. After a witness recovered from the shock, they often remembered more details.

Jack was looking more suspicious daily, because he avoided photos and hid his family details, and now his disappearance. Everything suggested he was hiding. Or even that he planned to kill Molly.

After the interviews, Miguel asked Richard to speak to Sir Giles's personal assistant over the phone.

"We notified him of Molly's death via the British police. She wanted to speak to someone in English, to plan the visit."

"Of course I will. Anything I can do to help."

The secretary was efficient and business-like in the way she talked.

"Please call me Geraldine. I organise things for Sir Giles. I recognise your name from the bombing in the London Museum and had heard you had a gallery on the Camino. I'm pleased that you are helping the local police because it will make my job easier."

This surprised him his location was not a secret, he couldn't imagine why she should be interested enough to remember.

"My flight to A Coruña is the day after tomorrow where I hire a car to drive to Sarria, arriving after midnight. I arranged this with the hotel. Sir Giles is flying the following morning, and I hired an automobile for him."

"Consider me at your disposal, both of you."

Geraldine was very unemotional in her response.

"He will appreciate your concern and the offer to meet him at the airport. Could you contact me at our accommodation once he has settled in instead?"

"Of course."

Although he didn't comment, he wondered why Sir Giles wanted to be the one to set the agenda.

A young local police officer promised Richard a lift home as he was due to begin the afternoon shift in the incident room. So he thanked Miguel and used the time in Sarria to buy groceries and eat something. Everything was surreal and the next few days unpredictable. He was glad to have an hour of unhurried domesticity.

His driver was eager to talk and was excited to be involved in a homicide enquiry, as no one could remember the previous murder. Richard understood how he felt.

There were several cars, both in his limited parking zone and the space further up the track owned by a neighbouring farmer. He was unused to the busyness, rarely seeing anyone other than the steady stream of pilgrims.

The sergeant asked where to store his canvases. The showroom was above his house and patio, the narrow stairs at the side of the building providing access to a storeroom beside his studio. It took an hour for four of them to move them all. During which, the team reassured him that this type of event was rare. It wasn't safety that worried him. It was how to get his paintings back on the gallery wall without help.

Without doubt, the extra exercise had exhausted him. His leg was painful, and he was in emotional turmoil. The realisation that the dead pilgrim was someone he knew upset him and brought back memories he assumed he had put behind him. He found it hard to call her Hambleton, even in thought, because he associated her with her father.

He hadn't remembered that she kept the name of her mother, a television actress who had died ten years ago. Only then had she moved to London to live with her estranged parent. Hardcastle introduced her to Richard as 'Molly, my daughter. They were alike, a matched pair and shared an effortless charm, an inability to look you in the eye, and the knack of appearing wherever a story unfolded. They were close and the different surnames jarred. He pictured her in her striking red evening dress at his medal presentation, her air of sophistication, the way she posed for photos, her immaculate hair. Was she the same girl who he saw arranged on his fence?

His mind was full of this as he sat with a sandwich and beer, his leg propped on a pillow. So grateful to rest that the sudden easing of the pain brought tears to his eyes, and he fell asleep before he finished the meal, head resting on the arm of the sofa. He dreamt of Gill and the happy times they had spent. The dream, as it often did, led to their last moments together, the Westminster exhibition, the terrorists planting the bomb. Gill in a pool of blood, an explosion, then nothing until he had woken up in the hospital. He wondered if he would repeat that period over in his dreams for the rest of his life.

In his dream, Sir Giles summoned him and told him that someone was planning to murder Molly and it was his duty to stop it from happening. A phone call from Miguel updating him interrupted his nightmare and saved him from a stiff neck caused by sleeping on the sofa.

The MP was arriving the day after tomorrow, Friday, on a scheduled flight. His secretary reaching Sarria in the early hours of Thursday to make the preparations. This was because her boss didn't want to fly via a budget airline. Richard thought this sounded like the arrangements for a business conference rather than a family tragedy.

He had spoken to Geraldine, the assistant, and offered his services and she accepted in the manner you might accept the duties of a concierge. Most fathers would have caught the first flight available, and the delay puzzled him, along with Sir Giles refusing a police driver.

Miguel phoned him with information and a request to go with him to meet the minister at his hotel. So they were both going.

As too many criminals escaped justice because the investigating officer didn't keep an open mind, he would wait until the meeting before forming an opinion.

At ten thirty, he poured himself a glass of wine and sat thinking about what he knew about the MP and the link between the bombing and Molly's death?

It couldn't be a coincidence, but wouldn't a terrorist organisation target Sir Giles not his daughter?

He needed to make several phone calls tomorrow if he wanted answers to these questions. Why did the Minister think the bombers targeted him? Richard racked his brains for memories.

Grief had filled his world. It had been in the papers, although he chose not to read the stories, so now he got out his notepad, drew up a search list and began work, and it was getting light outside by the time he finished.

Google led him to a variety of newspaper reports, and he was now better informed. Much of the information, though, was confusing. Although more tenuous links emerged from news articles, the only solid link between

Molly's murder and the bombings was him.

The press had ascribed the museum bombing to a terrorist attack perpetrated by Muslim extremists because Sir Giles had helped to negotiate controversial arms contracts with the Saudis.

Saudi Arabia's use of British armaments in the Yemen flouted international rules of war. They killed and displaced thousands of civilians in their attempt to rout out rebel forces. So was the incident linked and was it revenge?

Richard didn't know enough about middle eastern politics to be sure.

Two other news reports caught his eye. An organisation called the Russia Iran Business Association had invited sir Giles to a reception in London and a conference in Moscow, both of which he had attended.

The newspaper report described the association as *'a group of entrepreneurs from Russia and Iran'*.

Their aim was to stabilise oil prices by persuading America to remove economic sanctions on Iran. And by asking Britain to stop fuelling the war by selling weapons to Saudi Arabia. They then planned to help Iran and the Saudis to reinstate diplomatic relations and instigate peace talks in the Yemen, leading to world-wide stable pricing.

Then he read an interview with Professor Bonham, written in response to the museum bombing. The professor suggested Iran wanted to separate the Middle East from America and Britain and pave the way for a Muslim super-state strong enough to challenge the United States.

They planned to achieve this by creating an anti-western sentiment in the Muslim countries of the Middle East because terrorist attacks in western countries show intent and draw Muslim communities together with a common purpose.

Richard read the articles again because the scenario seemed far-fetched.

He had understood that Iran and Saudi Arabia have different views on Islam. The Saudis are Sunnis and the Iranians Shia. The Yemen war, in which the Saudis claimed the rebels are Iranian, has driven the states further apart, so why would they be working together against the west?

Only if you accept Iran handled the larger Muslim militias, including IS, does this make sense?

Russia's role remained unclear to Richard unless everything concerned oil and the demand for it.

But why Sir Giles who, despite having interests in several arms companies, was a minor player?'

Richard's head was aching. There were so many puzzle pieces he couldn't fit together.

Before now, he had found international high-risk games both distasteful and hard to grasp, as he had never been interested in either politics or wealth. However, this case fascinated him.

He went to bed in the early hours of the following day. This time, exhaustion won over his buzzing mind and it was nine thirty when the sun woke him. It streamed through the windows because he had forgotten to close the blinds.

# CHAPTER SEVEN

## *Richard learns more about Miguel*

The following morning, enjoying the freedom of having his own car, Richard hummed tunelessly as he drove. He appreciated being a detective again and arrived at the garrison two hours later than he had planned.

The first job was a visit to Triacastela, where he hoped he could collect a list of guests who had stayed in the same hostel, and interview the waiter in the restaurant where they had eaten the previous evening. Once organised, the guardia would keep going.

Finding Jack was next, and it was the same procedure where he set i everything up and then helped analyse the results when they came in to offer a time-line.

So, he spent the morning working out what questions he wanted the officers to ask.

It disappointed him not to be involved in the second phase of the investigation, as it meant individual queries and door-to-door interviews, and his Spanish was not that good yet.

In the past, his team's success depended on a meticulous method, not brilliance, and he had enjoyed the detail. Now he was on someone else's patch and it was their team doing the legwork and he wanted to be more involved in the action.

Whilst Miguel was sorting out details resulting from the statements to date, he asked if he could look round the base.

The young sergeant he had met the day before at the crime scene volunteered to escort him, stepping forward so fast that he suspected she had been waiting for the opportunity. Fortunately, she spoke enough English for them to understand each other.

The building enclosed a parade ground with offices to the front and barracks on the other two sides, staggered backwards towards the river. Now it was showing its age. Once much grander and designed to show strength, it struggled with the needs of a modern police force. The entire building smelt of dust, damp, cleaning fluid, and human occupation. Long ago, it housed more officers, but technology and the specialisation of law enforcement meant they needed fewer personnel.

The colonel belonged to a unit which dealt with international crime. He was based in Madrid but because of Galicia's connection with goods, especially drugs, smuggled from overseas; It made sense to have a local office.

It was a coincidence that Miguel was here when Richard discovered Molly's body, but as soon as they found out she was the daughter of an English government minister, he would have been informed,

Richard knew most of what she told him, but he enjoyed hearing a different perspective. And the young sergeant's pride at being connected with the judicial police touched him.

The station commander had assigned Elvira Gómez to the case, and she considered herself very fortunate in getting this level of experience.

Later that afternoon in Miguel's office, he thought his new friend looked tired. An adrenaline rush provides a burst of energy when you see the body lasting through the long night following discovery, but then the fatigue wins.

Miguel produced a scrap pad and a journal and placed them on his desk side by side. Richard raised his eyebrows.

"The black binder is official and if the court request, I offer it as evidence, but I always send a copy of my initial observations with the photos of the scene."

"And the brown?"

"Those pages I destroy as soon as I conclude my part in the investigation."

Richard used a similar technique, but he wondered why Miguel was making a point of it. He never admitted his procedure because he wanted the freedom to keep reminders to jog his memory and help his logic without affecting the argument. He hated sloppy detectives whose cases didn't even reach court because of personal prejudice and lack of evidence.

"I ask my squad to ensure that opinions are not mistaken for facts, or an officer's partisanship doesn't slip into the case notes," said Miguel.

"I understand, and I agree." Miguel was telling him not to be careless and that they expected him to work to the same standards as the judicial police.

He cast his mind back to his days as chief inspector when he was meticulous in insisting that they kept the team office clean of casual notes passed between officers in an investigation. Nothing was to get lost or go missing, that they treated evidence with care and they wrote working theories on the white-board. That was explained to each new officer.

When they met, Miguel said there were very few murders here, implying he was inexperienced.

The young English-speaking sergeant, who was so helpful in filling the details, suggested the colonel had more experience than anyone else in Spain. The man himself, after he had explained his job to Richard, had downplayed his ability, and that puzzled him.

'Sarria is his home town. Maybe it pays to have a modicum of humility where everyone knows you. Now he was assessing Richard's competence in working with his own team.

"So, what did you conclude from the interviews with the young couple?" Miguel inquired.

"Neither appeared to be lying and I would say that their grief was genuine. I believe they have more information than they have provided us so far. Sally seemed to hold something back."

"Do you consider that there is a direct involvement?" The colonel was watching him.

"Do you?" he asked, trying to hide his smile.

"Ah, my friend, you have seen through me. I suspect we think alike on this."

Richard noticed that even after having his bluff called, Miguel gave nothing away, the mark of an intelligent and experienced officer. He wanted this man's trust and hoped he offered it because despite the geniality, friendship wasn't there for the taking. Miguel was doing his job and, so far, doing it well.

In that case, we are colleagues now, so are you still prepared to help? Sir Giles might be happier dealing with a decorated British Police officer."

"Of course." The sparsity of words was an inadequate expression of the way his heart leapt at the prospect of being part of the investigation.

*Miguel.*

*The unit's investigations involved complex international politics, and he liked it that way. He rubbed his hands together. Now he was getting into his stride.* Miguel sensed Richard was as enthusiastic about the case as he was. Although his new friend was less expressive.

The commander had asked if he was prepared to visit the scene and, as he had heard stories of the English painter who discovered the body, he had agreed. He liked the artist/detective and now that he had seen his police record, realised that they had experiences in common. Besides, Carolina trusted him and with her infallible ability to see people's souls, he counted on her judgement.

The dead girl was the daughter of a politician, and that was enough to pique his interest. Then the possibility of middle-eastern, and even Russian involvement, put it into his jurisdiction. For now, he was keeping an open mind on the terrorist angle, but there were colleagues to call on if it was an unknown radical group.

The best thing was living at home and knowing the location. With a smile of anticipation, he sent for his team and found accommodation for them, requesting someone to remove everything from two more rooms for their use in the barracks. They also had the incident-room in Richard's gallery.

Despite this, he was nervous. He should have handed organisational control to Manuel as soon as his crew arrived here because Colonels don't get involved or visit the scene or lead meetings, but stay behind a desk. Of course trusted the squad leader, but preferred to be in the middle of everything. He loved having a 'go bag' ready to fly out of the country and embraced the long days and the camaraderie.

But he was in charge of an entire unit and its resources. Handling consultation requests was now the principal part of his job, and he needed to make time to do that from here. He likewise must handle appeals for help from the national police and other guardia units in Spain.

His promotion was on condition that he grew the department adding two or three new operational teams available. More and more crime was international and came within his remit. The task load stretched the existing team in too many directions and must expand. he worried about ending up with paperwork and a headache each day. So he pushed away the suspicion that being involved in the action and being an impartial overseer didn't mix. He wanted to be both a foot soldier and the guy on the plane drawing the map.

Soon, Sir Giles, the girl's father, arrives, he thought, hoping that once he had met him, he could assess what implications came with the murder. His team could handle the international diplomatic details. I wondered if it was a simple case where her boyfriend killed her after a domestic argument. Whatever happened, the MP and his assistant held the key, so Miguel left for home only two hours after he had said goodbye to Richard.

# CHAPTER EIGHT

## *Sir Giles Hardcastle*

It was mid-morning on Friday when Sir Giles Hardcastle gazed out over the carousel, looking for his luggage. The place was enormous but, to his annoyance, no one hurried. There wasn't a staff member available, and he was irritated by having to do this himself. He could see the baggage conveyor turning, but no cases had appeared.

He needed a drink and a chance to freshen up. Leaning on the trolley, he noticed creases in his suit and flicked at them with irritation. He couldn't imagine travelling in anything other than a jacket, preferring the formal wear which marked him out as someone of importance, especially as he travelled first class.

When he flew with Geraldine, his assistant (she objected to being called secretary), there was an intern willing to fetch and carry for the privilege of being with them.

Today, he was on his own. No upper class, and business was a single seat in the plane's front and a paper cup of coffee, not a separate, more comfortable section. His PA assured him she had booked hotel accommodation and liaised with the local plods. Her job should be to help him, not 'liaise'. Unless he asked her to, of course. He wished women would return to doing as they were told.

His daughter angered him coming to such a godforsaken place, although he didn't believe that he could lose his girl, who was always so full of life. He was sure that the murdered girl was an ordinary young woman, not his Molly. She didn't go hiking: it was so wrong. Someone else must have used Molly's identity because he couldn't think of her as dead. It overwhelmed him whenever he allowed himself to contemplate it, so be didn't.

Because his mind was elsewhere, he missed his suitcase and had to chase it round the carousel in a most undignified manner. He decided his assistant was to blame. She knew he needed her and he paid her to be here with him, not gallivanting on ahead.

Hence, when he emerged blinking into the bright arrivals room, he bought coffee and pastries. Geraldine never let him imbibe caffeine and cake, for which he had a weakness, on health grounds. This minor act of defiance cheered him enormously.

He had refused the offer of a driver, wanting to meet the detective on his own terms. In addition, he had spoken to Scotland Yard and insisted that they send someone competent to solve the case.

No, he planned to settle in his hotel, take a shower, and then greet the police officer there. Geraldine arranged everything, and he forgot his irritation and relaxed. At least she had rented a comfortable car and organised what he needed.

The high-end Mercedes came with good GPS navigation. The road was narrow and winding and he encountered little traffic, but Sir Giles was irritated by the rolling hills, the blossom on trees that edged the fields and the roads and the copper-and-lime-tinged woodland in the distance. For most people, driving through the rural landscape was soothing, but he didn't belong in this world and he couldn't imagine his daughter here, alive or dead.

The motorway, when he reached it, was empty, and the journey uneventful and swift. The quiet thrum of the mighty motor as he accelerated calmed him. Although many individuals enjoy birdsong or whale sounds, for him, nothing competed with the sound of a well-tuned engine.

Sarria was not a place he planned to visit, no historic charm and an inadequate hotel. Geraldine had booked him a suite, which was at least practical, if not comfortable. The visit started badly when he shared the lift with people wearing hiking boots, and he worried that the dining room would be full of people in walking gear. He shuddered at the lack of decorum and wished someone had told them to dress appropriately. Sadly, with no assistant available, he contented himself with standing with his back to them so that they couldn't start a conversation.

To avoid the inappropriate footwear in the restaurant, he ordered his late lunch from room service and had a shower, finishing just as Geraldine knocked on his door.

Now refreshed, he felt more generous, so, apart from a brief mention of the unsatisfactory journey, he made no complaint.

"The hotel has offered us a private lounge downstairs to meet the police," she said.

"Have they found who was impersonating Molly?" he asked.

His assistant looked at him in amazement.

"There is no question of impersonation. It is your daughter. I know that for a fact."

But Sir Giles was still shaking his head in disbelief as they reached the lift.

Spring in Galicia is glorious or terrible. Sometimes the weather gods scoop the Atlantic Ocean, and fling it on the countryside, not as drops in the wind or drizzle, but as a deluge. Water pours from the heavens and tumbles down the mountains; it blocks the roads, fills the many rivers, and finds every crack in the roof of your house. It saturates the clothes on your back as if God wants no part of you to be dry. Rubber boots and umbrellas are the most basic of necessities. Huge waterproof ponchos help those poor souls who need to be out. The best defence is a fire, a book and a glass of *aguardiente*.

That Friday afternoon, when Richard was due to meet Sir Giles, Galicia was putting on a show. A police driver collected him in a four by four, necessary to reach the main road. Spectacular streaks of lightning accompanied them into Sarria, and surface water suggested that they might have been quicker in a boat.

He had abandoned formal clothing in favour of warmth and wore a thick sweater with his smart flannel trousers, choosing a weatherproof jacket and boots instead of the blazer he had planned.

As he left, he glanced at his armchair and the log-burning stove, feeling their pull.

He wasn't looking forward to the meeting. Sir Giles had insisted it took place at his hotel, putting him in control with the police officers as his guests, an action more typical of a politician than a grieving parent.

He was still unsure why Miguel wanted him involved

in the meeting because his knowledge of British culture and language were as good as his own. He had grown up in London. Miguel was playing games.

Did he surprise Sir Giles or put him on edge? Conversely, his involvement hadn't surprised Geraldine. She expected it and must have discussed his presence with her boss by now, so it shouldn't shock Sir Giles either, but he was sure he had detected an undercurrent, something he wasn't being told.

He might think they brought Richard in to help him because of their earlier connection in London, so Miguel could then work without scrutiny. That must be Miguel's reasoning.

The rain was being forced into rivulets along the windowpane of the car and the wind forced it into complex patterns, reminding him of what they faced. Were they being pushed by outside forces to act in a predetermined way?

The hiker's death wasn't the entire story. It couldn't be.

He had avoided politics as much as he could in his police career, always working on the assumption money, revenge, or passion caused murder. Ninety-nine times out of a hundred, he was right. The cleanest explanation was often the correct one. But he had never dealt with high-profile crimes. There was a special team for that, so any hint of political intrigue or international criminal enterprise, and he handed everything over, grateful that it wasn't his to handle.

The simplest solution here was that the boyfriend killed Molly and then disappeared. But that didn't resolve why the murderer staged the body or his own connection with the government minister.

With that in his thoughts, they arrived at the hotel. He

noted, with internal satisfaction, that although it was Sarria's best, it wasn't up to Sir Giles' usual five star standard. 'Petty, ' he said to himself. 'Keep an open mind, don't get drawn into personalities.'

The rain soaked both him and his driver in the two minutes it took to run from the car park to the lobby. After a quick word with the receptionist, she disappeared into the bar in search of a hot drink for the chauffeur. While they waited, Richard removed his wet coat.

When she returned, she hung up Richard's jacket and directed him to a small private lounge where he saw Miguel and Sir Giles. To his surprise, the local policewoman, Ana, whom he had met on the first day, was with them. He remembered they had co-opted her to be an interpreter, but wondered why they needed her today.

The colonel introduced them in *Gallego,* the language of Galicia. It surprised Richard, although he was careful to keep his reaction to himself. Ana, the officer, interpreted the introduction. But when he spoke again, it was in broken English.

"But you people know each other already."

He stepped forward to shake hands, but Sir Giles was staring with disdain at Richard's footwear.

When the MP heard his name, he looked up abruptly, his frown turning to confusion.

"The Westminster bombing," Richard said, and his expression changed.

"Chief Inspector Harris, the hero who saved the day. Are you here because of that? I heard you moved to Spain, but I assumed you'd gone to the Costas for a bit of sun.... A chance to grieve the loss of your wife."

"I was hoping to escape from police work."

"Señor Harris found your daughter outside his cottage,"

said Miguel, this time in Spanish.

"Did you recognise her then? How can it be Molly? She doesn't do these outdoor sports and although I know she came with her friends, she always took taxies at home, so how could she walk here?" The eagerness on his face was childlike, and Richard hated to extinguish his hope.

"The doctor has checked her DNA and fingerprints. I am so sorry, but we are certain it's your daughter, but of course, you will wish to see her for yourself."

Sir Giles appeared not to hear him.

"Stepping in to help the local boys eh, not to worry, I've a chief Inspector coming over from Scotland Yard. I want this solved, you understand, and she is very good."

Miguel looked at Richard, who by now had realised that his new colleague was playing the simple country police officer.

"I will be here to ensure she gets all the cooperation she needs."

Sir Giles perplexed him. He appeared to think that he had no role other than helping him. Was it grief or disbelief that stopped him from seeing a more sinister connection? Or had Miguel's play acting created the scenario where he became Sir Giles's confidant?

"Earlier I put out a call for information regarding Molly's bodyguard, but we didn't know about him until this morning," Miguel was speaking via the interpreter.

"And Jack is missing also? Where is this place, the wild west? The terrorists must have removed the private detective and Jack before they got to Molly?"

"Bodyguard?"

So he had expected a problem.

"Seemed sensible to hire one. Geraldine has all the details."

Richard nodded, but said nothing aloud because he needed to position himself as Sir Giles's friend and the trustworthy English hero.

The panic grew in Sir Giles. His shoulders tensed and the rising pitch of his voice at the realisation that the victim might be his daughter. That was it. He hadn't behaved as a grieving parent because he didn't believe that she was dead. In his mind, it was a cruel joke or identity theft.

"If you wish, you can see Molly now?" he said.

He hoped the colonel was ready, as it was late in the day, but Miguel nodded reassuringly.

"There is protection arranged for you here at the hotel, and I have informed your own security team of the arrangements so they can send people to assist. The terrorist organisation may still be here."

The two officers, looking after Sir Giles, were chosen for their size and wearing military uniforms and side-arms emphasised their bulk.

They impressed the man.

At the prospect of seeing Molly, his bullish demeanour had slipped, and he looked vulnerable and alone.

Richard had seen this before, and briefly grasped sir Giles' shoulder.

Once you saw the body of your loved one, everything became real. Powerful men broke, even hostile ones. Then, after the funeral, the grief settled. The long agonising days and nights, the inability to cope with the smallest thing.

He tried to catch Geraldine's eye as he left, meaning to ensure that she was co-ordinating, but as she was watching Sir Giles, a smile of satisfaction flickered across her face at Sir Giles's growing distress, and it kept him silent.

# CHAPTER NINE

## *Richard in danger*

They spent the next few minutes sorting out transport, finding drivers for Sir Giles and Geraldine, and making sure that everyone learnt how to contact each other. Amid this, Miguel leaned over to Richard and said.

"We need to talk, La Parisien, this evening. I'll message." He nodded, wondering how he was going to get home.

The bar suggested was famous for its tapas and favoured by locals. It was busy throughout the year and didn't attract many tourists, perfect for a private conversation. The weather was foul outside, and dusk approached, so with an hour to kill, he found somewhere to sit in comfort with a coffee.

When he emerged, the dark had deepened. In the country, he often watched the stars from his cottage, the Milky Way snaked like a veil across the sky, and the constellations were so visible they looked to be within reach, but he could see no stars in town. He pulled up his hood and fastened his coat before he raced, as much as his limp allowed, through the streets.

Sarria is small and nowhere is far. The flats tower above the shops and bars, and so the roads appear narrow and gloomy without sunshine. By now residents had closed their shutters and scurried out of the rain, and the neighbourhood felt closed.

The water had seeped through his coat when he arrived at La Parisien and the warmth inside held a muggy humidity. The bright bar contrasted with the street and there was a buzz of conversation but few seats,however, he bagged a table from someone leaving. It was beside the pellet burner that heated the entire room. Then he ordered a glass of wine and hoped that Miguel planned to drive him home.

He sipped his drink and ate his *tapas* and considered reasons the colonel had played the role of an inept country police officer again? Was it his way of weighing people? If so it slowed progress although individuals made unguarded comments when they expected the professional was elsewhere.

Richard had talked to colleagues in Interpol, and they recognised Colonel Lopez as an expert on international crime based in Madrid, although he spent time in Barcelona and overseas.

Why meet in a bar? Although maybe it shouldn't surprise him, because most of his neighbours carried out business transactions in bars, face-to-face conversation helped to hire a plumber or a builder. Why not a police officer?

Geraldine knew where he lived, and that puzzled him. She had learnt that this case involved him, but hadn't told her employer and he remembered her expression when Sir Giles realised Molly was dead and was sure she had enjoyed that moment.

Molly's father was more difficult, seeming smaller than Richard recalled, and less confident of himself. He didn't understand the man's reaction to Molly's death, although in his experience, it was better to wait until grief took hold. Now he realised what caused him to doubt that Sir Giles was the target of the Westminster bombing. There was not enough substance, and he was mainly bluster and talk and not the brains behind the scenes. Further, he wasn't popular or influential and so not worth singling out by a terrorist group when there were more obvious targets.

Who wanted to kill Sir Giles, if anyone? Or was he too focused on his own importance?

Richard twitched with frustration because his internet search hadn't given him enough information on the complex politics and he needed to learn more.

This mind was on all these things when Miguel arrived, slipping in beside him and ordering alcohol free beer and food for them both.

"Would it be possible for you to move into the barracks?"

That was a surprise.

"Why and where?" he asked, alarmed. "I know your team has moved from Madrid. How big is the campus, and why? The incident room is in my gallery, so I can't run away."

"No, I'm worried they may kill you. There is an apartment for officers."

"What makes you think that I'm in danger?"

"It's complicated."

"I was wrong about Sir Giles?"

"No, you were wrong about Molly."

Richard raised his eyebrows in question, but Miguel shook his head so he assumed that meant not here, and changed the topic.

"Any news from the house to house?"

"We have enough information to build a timeline. There are descriptions of pilgrims travelling alongside them and a witness to the argument they had, and someone who saw Jack later that day."

"And the bodyguard?"

"The not very competent private detective used by Sir Giles. Yes, we have found him. You can meet him tomorrow." The officer was smiling, and the bar was emptying.

"I'm afraid that some of my team broke into your house and packed a bag for you. It is in your new room."

"I haven't agreed yet," he objected.

"It was never a question," said Miguel, his smile turning into laughter.


Later, on the short drive to the barracks, they continued the conversation.

"It devastated sir Giles when he saw the body of his daughter. He seemed to collapse in on himself."

Richard nodded because he had seen this happen often.

"Sometimes people are in denial until we force them to face reality," he replied.

"He lost his bluster and self-importance and confessed he had been receiving death threats. They had been arriving by post and email for months meant to intimidation both himself and his family."

"Didn't he receive threatening letters before the bombing at the London Museum?" asked Richard, who remembered one of the newspaper articles mentioned it.

"They were very similar," replied Miguel. "And so now we have an established link between the two events. In that instance, they continued for a year, and targeted both him and his family. The threats came from a group called the IRA. Iran, Russia, Alliance, not the Irish Republican Army, but with the same initials."

"Why were they targeting Sir Giles? What was the connection there?"

"None that we recognise, although he has links with a Business Association known as RIBA, also to do with Russia and Iran, not Muslim, not political, so not our organisation. It's a strange coincidence, and they knew all about him.

He reported the letters to the police, but the messages stopped after the bombing. He received threats for three months. Scotland Yard is sending out the officer in charge of that entire case."

"Inspector Jane Landis?" asked Richard.

"Chief Inspector, today. What can you tell me about her?"

Richard paused.

"Not much. I have never worked with her," he said.

"But?"

" Decide when you meet."

"Well, you have sidestepped me twice and so I guess you don't like her."

By now, he was glad that Miguel couldn't read face or body language in the dark car.

"In my experience, she is very ambitious, both socially and on the job. A couple of my team worked for her before they joined me. I'm prepared to say nothing else."

"OK, no more questions. There is more about my interview with Sir Giles to tell you."

"Yes," said Richard. He disliked Jane Landis, for more reasons than he wanted to mention.

Two junior officers came to him from her department. They were both Muslim, both with complaints of incompetence and insubordination in their files. But he found them excellent detectives, and he suspected that their religious and ethnic origins had caused the problem.

According to gossip, she mixed with officials of a higher grade, but only those who enjoyed a particular reputation that smelled of corruption. None of this was provable, but he didn't trust her in London, and nothing inclined him to trust her now.

"Sir Giles admitted that because he hired a private investigator to look after her, he struggled to believe that Molly was dead. He found it hard to accept that she would walk the Camino because she liked her comforts and wasn't sporty. When she told him, he imagined her staying in *Paradores* and travelling by car. He had met Jack, didn't like him, and had written him off as a social climber." He had carried on talking whilst Richard's mind was on Jane Landis.

"Sir Giles wanted to wait for the Scotland Yard detective before mentioning the death threats. So he likes her. His assistant insisted he talked to me at once, in case the information proved urgent."

The next task was to learn about the IRA. Once again, his new friend shook his head imperceptibly, as if to show that they shouldn't discuss it here. It was the second time he had done that.

"I would like to talk about the private investigator," said Richard, unsure whether Miguel wanted to share that information with him, either.

"Good, so would I."

The conversation was getting stilted. In fact, it sounded as though it came from a Pink Panther movie.

They discussed the bodyguard who was being interviewed in the morning. But too many late nights and too much disturbed sleep was taking its toll, and he couldn't concentrate.

Miguel invited him home the following evening for dinner and he hoped it was to give him more information.

Miguel showed him to a tiny apartment. His bag was there, and someone had stocked the kitchen. A security badge and a canteen card lay on the table. The canteen had a hatch and two vending machines, but the woman in charge had grandiose ideas.

His sketchpad was on the desk with pencils and watercolour pastels and a note telling him to *sketch what he remembered*. Besides that, his laptop, tablet, and e-book reader and a note explaining the reading material'.

Sure enough, someone had added several documents to his device. This was not a holiday then.

The apartment comprised one large room divided into three sections. There was a bathroom, bedroom, and living space, cosy, private, and on the first floor.

Miguel asked him not to leave the barracks, and to be cautious even indoors, ensuring that he locked his windows and doors. In addition, no one could visit without prior arrangement. It was alarming, and it frightened him if was being considered a genuine threat.

In twenty years on Serious Crimes, he had never been in real danger. There was no threat to his life. The action that won him the bravery medal was a calculated risk to save a child. On that occasion, he was in control and he had got involved by choice. He ran away from trouble, but it still found him. Miguel indicated he was planning to tell him more, but not here. Being helpless was not good because it reminded him of being in hospital recovering from the damage to his leg. Everyone else made decisions for him and he hadn't liked it then either.

It was dark outside, so he closed the shutters and prepared coffee, fumbling around the tiny kitchen to find what he required. While the espresso was brewing, he unpacked his bag and put everything away, noticing he lacked clothes for longer than a few days.

He looked through the documents. At home, he never drank caffeine this late, but both his plight and the nightmares he had been having unnerved him, so occupying his mind should settle his thoughts. But he needn't have worried about the caffeine as his coffee remained untouched on the table and his paperwork slipped to the floor. He slept for so long that he missed the start of the interview with the private detective on Saturday morning.

# CHAPTER TEN

## *Cloak and Dagger*

An officer showed Richard into the observation room and handed him a set of headphones. One of Miguel's team was there, and he pointed to a seat to watch Miguel and Manuel's interview on a screen. The introductions were happening when he arrived.

The private sleuth wore chinos and a polo shirt and looked as though police interviews were routine. As the detective wasn't a suspect, the tone was friendly although they queried his failure to protect Molly.

"The failure happened because she assumed I was stalking her. Normally, the target knows I'm there and what my role is. After a couple of days, they ignore me and I do my thing. I explained how it worked, and that on an extensive project, keeping hidden was impossible and could reduce my chances. The client was insistent. I wanted to pull out, but my boss insisted because we were getting paid a bundle and it was an easy gig. So yes, I failed and I'm sorry. I'll carry the can because I should have pulled out."

"Miss Hardcastle 'carried the can'." Miguel's voice was sharp.

Dave Bromley nodded, but said no more.

"Could you give a list of suspicious people or anyone you saw frequently?"

"There are comprehensive notes in my room. But from memory, Molly contacted three separate groups of individuals. She told companions that they were relatives of her mothers.

Otherwise, I remember seeing a man with a dog. I chatted with him and he said the animal was a stray he found in the mountains. The woman in a green coat who wore black leggings and a silk scarf which covered part of her face and she never removed the coat. That's why I noticed her. The fabric was that breathable material that walkers often wear. She often stopped in the same town or village. There was a couple who met them for dinner on several occasions."

Miguel and Manuel asked a few more questions, but Dave Bromley referred them back to his notes, which they hadn't allowed him to bring into the interview.

"Can we have your photos?"

"No photos, orders of the client. Yes, it was a mistake to take the case when the client's wishes hampered my chances of success."

Why did Sir Giles restrict the project? Dave Bromley hadn't stood a chance.


Richard hoped Miguel might explain the cloak and dagger stuff, and he was not disappointed. At six o'clock that evening, as dusk was falling, he was sitting in a deckchair in a poly-tunnel heated by an ancient paraffin heater.

Carolina gave him a fleece blanket to drape over his knees, and he held a glass of whisky, presented by his new colleague. The solar-powered garden lights offered just enough light to see.

"My friend, I am sorry for this. But we have received intelligence that Jack and Molly were agents for a dangerous group. A group wanting to escalate the unrest in the Middle East, but also to stir up hate against Muslims in the West.

At this stage, we are positive of very little except they may offer arms and funds to radical Islamic groups to spark trouble, but more information is coming every day. Somehow, details of our investigation are reaching them.

I want to interview the people described by the private detective. The woman with the green coat may be one of their group. Many pilgrims find dogs, but he might have seen something if we can track him down."

"And there is that couple who insisted on joining them for dinner."

"Witnesses have mentioned the woman in green several times. So did Sally James," said Miguel.

"Also, why did Sir Giles put restrictions on a bodyguard?" he asked.

"He may be trying to find an excuse for failing, so we'll check his contract. Molly refused a bodyguard and her father didn't want her to know, so it was a clandestine job."

"So Molly asked Mr Bromley to help lift an injured pilgrim's bag onto the bus. Where was the driver?" Richard asked.

"Helping an old lady up the step."

"It sounds innocent, since they ate breakfast in the bar

closest to the bus stop. Then the server told him Jack and Molly had left for Samos." Richard was trying to imagine the scene.

"Yes, I found the waiter this afternoon, and a woman gave him five euros to pass on that message," said Miguel.

"Why did Dave Bromley believe him?"

"The group planned to visit the monastery in Samos. He listened to them talking about it the previous night and overheard Sally agree to change their route to the shorter one because they wanted to give the couple a few days' space."

" So you think Molly left the message, and she was giving him the slip?" asked Richard.

"The description fits."

"So, either they were after Jack, or wanted them both, and he escaped. Another possibility is the boyfriend murdered her to get at Sir Giles," said Richard.

"An indirect attack on the minister might be a distraction or a practice run."

"If she was with a terrorist group, could she be a target?"

"It's possible that the couple fell out over how to proceed. We need more information before we discard anything."

"Is Sir Giles cleverer than we are giving him credit for? In which case, his blustering is hiding a sharper political mind with an unseen agenda?" Richard said.

Miguel sighed before he spoke next, frowning as he thought things through.

"Too little knowledge can be dangerous and we lack evidence."

"So what now?"

"Assume there are listening devices and be circumspect

in what you say. My team is working on countermeasures and clearing personnel. The expert arrived this morning."

"It sounds melodramatic, but is your home not safe?" Richard asked, not knowing how concerned he should be?

Miguel was laughing now.

"Of course, my house is secure, but I hoped you might appreciate the drama of sitting here amongst the plants."

He looked at his friend and then joined in the laughter.

"Bloody Hell, you worried me so much." The colonel had broken the tension and cemented their friendship.

"Do you want to go indoors?" Miguel said.

The man was laughing so much he almost spilled his drink.

"Not if you have brought the bottle of whisky out with you," he replied.

His new comrade poured them both another glass.

"There is danger, and it is better to be prudent, even though I appreciate my suspicions are overkill, but your home is not safe at night."

"We continue the investigation as if it were a domestic murder, Jack being a suspect. We suspect Tom and Sally because they haven't told us everything they know."

"What of Sir Giles and his death threats?"

"We deal with those. The British police are aware of them and they are on record."

"And the group, the IRA?"

"More difficult because they may not exist. "

"And myself?" Richard was grinning.

"In public, you are not above suspicion and you staying at the barracks will help that belief. I have been obtuse about your reasons for being there because you may be in danger because of a link between you and the murder. In addition, someone killed Molly outside your house and they intended you to find her. I'm sure it is not foul play on your part and Spanish intelligence thinks so too... and the CIA and MI5... and Carolina."

Miguel's face lit up with a gigantic smile.

"Of course, my wife is never wrong... And I have clearance for you to join my squad. My team knows. However, we cannot afford to make it open yet, so please forgive the guardia and the local police for not taking you into their confidence. "

"You are sure information is being leaked?"

"Yes, but you can trust my unit, who have been tested over time, but someone could bribe other personnel."

Richard focused on reasons he might be a target. This was his first multi-national investigation and if it wasn't so personal, he might enjoy the challenge.

There was a companionable silence, mellowed by the whisky. The danger was not immediate, and that reassured him, although it was real and frightening. Miguel's joke suggested he had gained his trust, and he appreciated that. He was enjoying a pleasant evening with friends, a rare pleasure. It felt like he was waking from a dream. When he lost Gill, he suspended his life, and now it was starting again.


Sir Giles changed from being demanding to being apologetic. He was out of his depth and asked relentless questions and was sure that the British police would swoop in and solve everything.

He told Miguel the inspector had the qualifications and the information, and Richard could confirm that. The colonel, in the meantime, insisted on speaking through an interpreter and asking basic questions as though he were an inexperienced local officer.

Richard guessed his friend had played this role before and watched with interest. Hardcastle equated Englishness with ability, so he offered many theories, which he explained at great length. Richard needed to keep reminding himself to give the man leeway, as he had just lost his daughter, but his stock of patience was being tested.

Geraldine Brown, the MP's assistant, was a calming influence and a conduit of information. She knew every detail on her boss's schedule for the last ten years. Through her, Miguel's team built up a picture of his associates and their whereabouts. They hoped to find the terrorist link and reason Sir Giles or his daughter might be a target.

Each move was being passed on and potential witnesses vanished, or changed their minds, before the colonel interviewed them. Sometimes leads fizzled out, and on one occasion crime-scene photos disappeared. They locked the physical evidence away, but it worried Miguel and made everyone uneasy.

Meanwhile, local interviews continued, and he hoped that sheer persistence might turn something up. They needed something break the case.

They interviewed Tom and Sally again, and now they had recovered from the first shock, they remembered more details and could see people's ulterior motives.

"There was a couple who wanted to eat dinner with us, so we often ate as a group. Everyone has a story to tell. This pair, though, were different, turning up more often than other pilgrims, suggesting that as they were from Sheffield, they were almost neighbours."

Tom said that they irritated him most when he wanted a quiet meal with his girlfriend.

They noticed the woman in the green coat because she

avoided talking to them.

Sally confessed that her friend's stalker worried them and that Molly argued with Jack about him. The guy stayed in a nearby hostel from the beginning. Same thing when they ate. They noticed he was always on his own in the next restaurant. Molly told her she had a way to avoid stalkers, and it was in character for Molly to set a trap and try to teach him a lesson. In addition, she insisted that Tom and Jack weren't told because she thought they might overreact.

These were minor details, which could prove useful. The couple, having shared their grief with Sir Giles, booked flights home to Sheffield; as they were no longer suspects, Miguel let them go suggesting that they wrote a list of everything they knew about Molly to offer him at their final interview before their flight.

Richard, in his room, read what he could on Iran, Russia and the relationship with Saudi Arabia. The more he learnt, the less he liked the information. The more he discovered, the more he understood the complexity.

His limited experience dealing with either complicated or politically motivated crimes concerned him.

Everything that he had read, or uncovered, suggested that this murder wasn't the work of an individual working alone. Someone was acting as part of a team and driven by a cause. That put it outside his experience.

But he wanted to help, so to understand the order of events, he followed his old routine of laying everything out and asking the obvious questions that arose. He wanted to be useful to Miguel and needed to start somewhere.

Jack?

Who was he? Did he belong to a terrorist organisation?

Where was he? Why had he disappeared? Why did no one who met him warm to him?

He is the boyfriend, but who else is he?

Tom Miller appeared to be everything he had said he was.

Sally?

Lived with Tom, no children. Normal. The information she had been withholding concerned the stalker. It could have been Dave Bromley, the private investigator hired as a bodyguard.

She was a university friend of Molly's and he was sure Sally knew more about her earlier activities, so it be worth asking more questions.

Sir Giles?

Was he an ambitious buffoon?

Did he have any political connections with groups or individuals who benefited from his downfall?

Did he have threatening connections dangerous enough to harm him?

Was the bomb in the London museum intended for him? Was Molly's death designed to hurt her father?

Geraldine, Sir Giles's assistant?

No genuine need to ask questions. They did a background check and found she was single and lived alone. She had done the job for ten years.

Richard *marked* her name because something was not right.

Private Detective Dave Bromley.

Worked for Brooks and Brooks with a valid licence and Sir Giles paid for him from his individual funds. Jack and Molly had spotted and outflanked him. Was he competent at his job? Possibly not, but that wasn't a crime, and he gave a detailed statement.

Woman in green?

As yet unidentified, seen by the private detective and one other pilgrim.

Mystery couple?

Himself?

How was the bomb at the London museum linked? Was he involved? Did they think he held important information?

If so, what did he know?

He still didn't understand why someone wanted to kill Molly at all. Why outside his house? Why the grotesque staging?

Stabbed through the heart sounded professional, but may have been lucky.

Two probable reasons for the argument; She had discovered Jack was hiding something. They spotted Dave Bromley and disagreed on how to give him the slip, or even if they needed to.

Why was the question? Why?

# CHAPTER ELEVEN

## *The other Chief Inspector*

DCI Jane Landis flew to Galicia on the Monday after the murder. Much to Richard's delight, Sergeant John Hollis, an old colleague of his, accompanied her.

He was an interesting choice of companion for Jane. Richard knew him to be a long serving, honest detective, with a great deal of experience dealing with homicide cases, and not at all the colleague he had imagined she would choose.

She was a desk person, leaving her inspectors to do the legwork with their teams, but slick at negotiating with the press and top management. Richard had always wondered how easy it was to serve with her. He suspected she was manipulative with peers and dismissive of lower ranks.

They had mixed in different social circles and had distinct interests in the office. She was an inspector when he left the force, but everybody was aware she was ambitious. He doubted she intended to stop soon.

John, a veteran police officer, was an odd decision for

her bagman. When he was on Richard's team, he was a solid, methodical detective. He had told Richard that DS was his desired rank and had never changed his mind, claiming that if 'everyone went for promotion, no one who was not wet behind the ears would be working.' He was neither smooth nor political and had worn the same rumpled suit since he shifted to plain clothes. Or if he had traded suits, there was no distinction between old and new. He avoided being sent back to uniform, the fate of the unambitious officer in CID. By solid police work, he got on with everyone and made himself indispensable.

Miguel and Richard were collecting them, and he was glad of a trip out. The barracks were sending him stir crazy, and he didn't want to stay much longer.

Never having been interested in cars, buying a more expensive model had felt alien, but it kept him independent. The company fitted out the top-end of the range model for off-road expeditions, incidentally, making them suitable for disabilities like his own. The automatic transmission and custom handbrake together with the pull-out step and handles all came as standard, and he loved everything about it. He volunteered to play chauffeur.

He enjoyed driving and did everything he could to ensure that he could continue safely. Since his injury, he was terrified of becoming dependent and losing control.

The weekend's heavy rain had cleared to a silver tinted mist, but once the sun burned through, it would be strong. Galicia is a place of moods, brooding, stormy and angry, mysterious, glorious in its brightness, unbearable in its oppressive heat. Like the wild horses that roamed the mountain areas, unpredictable, unbreakable, with a charm as enticing as a siren.

He used his GPS to find the colonel's house. The roads

here played games with even the best sense of direction, winding through hills and forests with nothing to distinguish them as different. The mists rolled in and out, ghosts of the silent trees and ancient houses.

Richard arrived just as the sun broke through the cloud. Through the trees, he could still see mist hovering over the river. The early morning light bathed the dwelling, the pale grey granite sparkling where the rays hit the crystalline rock. The day was alive with the possibilities.

The colonel waited, looking more like a country farmer than a police officer. He changed his boots for shoes and put on his suit jacket, then he drank the coffee that was made for him. They set off in good spirits. He looked forward to a day out and Miguel was genial and chatty.

The journey was neither long nor arduous. Rush hour does not exist in rural Galicia, and on a sunny day, driving is nothing but pleasant. They chatted about life in the Met, and his colleague asked his opinion of Jane Landis. He grinned and repeated what he said on the earlier occasion. He told him about John Hollis.

"So, you don't trust her. Why not?"

It was a statement, not a question, and true. He distrusted her, but he didn't gossip either. Working with her might change his mind, and if it didn't, then he would have personal experience on which to base his opinion.

The investigation was going well, and if it worried Miguel having even more English police involved, there was nothing to show it.

They were both concerned that Jack Clark had vanished without a trace. Customs hadn't scanned his passport, so it was unlikely that he had returned to the UK. At least not by conventional means. Either he was the killer, and part of a well-linked group, or dead himself. Miguel felt that the longer he was missing, the less chance of it being domestic or straight-forward. Someone had watched the pair leaving Triacastela together and Richard's house was only three kilometres away.

Miguel's team hadn't located the woman in green or the friendly couple.

People had seen them, either dining or walking, and one pilgrim sat with them in a bar one night before joining them for the evening meal, but hadn't seen them since. Nobody offered their names or their current location.

The same with the woman in green. They saw her but didn't know her whereabouts.

It's important to rule out what can't have happened first. A clearer picture emerges as the team clears away the mud and debris which clouds everyone's life. So, finding Jack and narrowing the motives were this week's priorities. They both hoped the new chief Inspector had extra information for them.

On Monday, the ninth of April, one week after someone had killed Molly Hardcastle, Jane Landis unconsciously straightened her hem as they walked down the plane steps. She took particular care of her appearance because she never dressed for herself she was only interested in the effect of her image on other people. Today she wore slim-fit trousers, which flattered her even after a plane journey. A fitted jacket over a silk blouse kept her looking businesslike. In addition, a hint of cleavage and the drape of her shirt ensured she attracted the scrutiny of the surrounding men, while the distinctive quality and probable cost of her clothes got the attention of the women. She believed first impressions to be important, so she always made certain that the impression counted.

Behind her, she could hear Gregory Bonham's carry-on bag bump on every step. It was his only ever flight on a budget airline, and his discomfort and obvious distaste amused her, making her journey more bearable. Her promotion to chief inspector ensured she didn't have to do this operational work often. Gregory's insistence on involving himself meant she needed to be here in person. They worked together well, but as she couldn't predict what he might say, he could compromise her position. Because she took a bigger risk than ever in clearing up the London Museum bombing, she was in danger of letting someone else jeopardise her career.

The passenger terminal lay before them, spacious and modern for such a small airport. She had expected a large barn, used more for freight because most flights were with budget airlines. She collected her suitcase, ignoring Gregory, and looked toward the double doors into the arrivals hall. He came up behind her, pushing a trolley, his case, and a carry-on bag dumped on top. You could class his luggage as vintage, she thought. Good brand, but not cared for properly. With a sigh, she wondered why the wealthy showed so little appreciation.

Jane, however, prided herself on making every penny count. Her clothes and baggage were secondhand, bought and restored because she preferred quality, and didn't buy what she didn't need. Since she teamed up with Gregory, he paid for most things and she let him because she wanted him to think he was her protector.

"My dear, let's see if our hosts have arrived, shall we? Can I take your bag?"

Still saying nothing, she turned and rearranged the trolley to protect her case, putting the handle back into Gregory's hands. She hated being called my *dear*, but now wasn't the time to object. They both ignored Sergeant

Hollis, who was struggling with his own cheap suitcase, together with two official briefcases, and the rucksack he used as a carry-on bag. Gregory pushed the baggage in his direction before following her out into the arrivals lounge. The cart overloaded, was impossible to push and difficult to steer, but Jane was oblivious to the struggle of underlings and blamed John for the five minutes it took him to haul the luggage through the crowded doorway.

They were at the airport on time and identifying the detective chief inspector was easy, as most other passengers were pilgrims. They were identifiable by their boots or walking sandals and huge rucksacks. To their surprise, there was someone else with her. An older man, very tall and thin, stooped, with white hair. He looked familiar, but Richard didn't place him until the introductions.

The Police woman stepped forward, holding out her hand.

"Colonel López, I'm Chief Inspector Jane Landis. Pleased to meet you."

She was small and neat, with dark hair tied back in a round bun, her short coat and trousers not rumpled by travel and her makeup minimal and professional.

"*Encantado.*" Miguel gave his most charming smile. "And your companion?"

"Professor Gregory Bonham, who has both information and expertise."

She looked at Richard but addressed her remarks to Miguel.

"Well, we are quite a party. Is there room in your car?"

Richard glanced around for John Hollis and realised he was struggling with a luggage trolley in the crowded doorway. The sergeant flashed him a grin when their eyes met, and he noted his friend looked even more rumpled than he remembered.

"I believe you know Richard Harris, who volunteered to drive and help with any cultural issues which may arise. Although I learnt my English in London, I remained very Spanish. I like to avoid any unnecessary misunderstandings when I can."

"Chief Inspector." Jane looked at him, waiting to see how he reacted to the title.

"Just Richard these days, a provincial artist." he said. Then smiled in what he hoped was a friendly fashion.

"Oh, but I understood they had co-opted you onto the case."

Richard had expected to follow Miguel's lead, wondering whether the bumbling local police officer or the inexperienced rural detective were on the cards. However, today, Miguel was every inch the colonel of a special operations unit with correct and formal English, and he was in total command of the scene.

"Indeed, he has, and you are right, of course, that in public we should use his rank. I apologise, Chief Inspector. The grave nature and the necessity to locate expert colleagues has caused me to slip up on protocol."

Miguel's remarks made Jane look pompous, and she blushed.

Miguel turned to the professor.

"Welcome to Galicia, sir, and thank you for your services. May I suggest we don't dawdle here in this draughty hall but find the car and then a restaurant where we can talk over lunch? There is no time to waste, though I understand you may be tired."

This Miguel was different again to the one he picked up

this morning, when anyone might mistake them for friends on a fishing trip.

The subtle power play continued through their meal, barely hidden by the amicable expressions on various faces.

Positioned at the end of the table alongside his old-time friend, John Hollis, the sergeant brought him up to date on the activities of former colleagues.

The friends listened to and watched the other characters even as they talked. The colonel was enjoying himself, playing the genial host in control. Jane was being smooth, flirting, dropping names of important people into her conversation, emphasising her department's successes. He guessed she was looking for promotion from this and assessing which techniques to use with Miguel, whose approval she needed.

The professor was the member of the party who surprised him. He was playing the humble academic, but Richard was positive it was an act. He kept throwing in challenges, testing the colonel's knowledge and understanding of political systems and asking innocuous questions regarding the perimeter of Miguel's jurisdiction.

Something was behind the questions, either trying to trick Miguel into giving away too much information or finding a weakness in Miguel's command of his unit?

He suspected the aristocrat and Jane knew each other better than suggested. He was unsure why Lord Gregory Bonham wasn't using his title.

He was a genuine academic, which is rare for the aristocracy. Also, the designer of the Westminster Exhibition, which Richard had saved from being bombed.

But he was a multimillionaire with a vast country estate just north of London and the thing that normally opened doors for him was his position as Duke of Southerby and his family's Royal connections.

Richard turned to his companion.

"What's your take on the professor?"

"Seems a nice old man, knows his stuff by the sound of it."

"And what does your gut say? If it's not too full of Galician steak and chips."

There was hesitation before the sergeant lowered his voice and spoke.

"Wouldn't trust him with a barge pole sir, the DCI is not likely to appreciate me saying that though."

"How about you tell the boss what she wants to hear, and let me know if instinct tells you different, just between us?"

John nodded as if Richard had said something significant.

Power play aside. By the end of lunch, they had briefed the newcomers on progress. Lord Bonham had claimed a reliable researcher had given him information that the original bombers had ties to an extremist Muslim organisation in Iran.

"But their families were British," said Richard.

"Muslims," corrected the professor.

"Indeed, I have letters and emails in my bag to show the colonel, suggesting the group has links to the IRA. Are you aware that Islam is an evangelical and radical religion?"

"While I don't have your knowledge of religions and their political affiliations, I know people are welcome to convert into the faith. However, I'm not sure what you mean by radical," Richard said.

The professor glanced at him, then turned away and

spoke to Jane, his eyes fixed on the top button of her blouse.

He was glad when they finished lunch. Certainly his friend enjoyed playing politics. He did not, nor did he intend to start. Still unsure what his task was here, he decided once they had settled everyone into their rooms; he needed a long conversation with Miguel. The games people played annoyed him. The colonel, with the dexterity of a Shakespearean actor, created a new role with every person he met and enjoyed it, frustrating Richard. He was a thinker, not a player, and days such as this exhausted him. By half-past six, they had checked the three newcomers in to their accommodation.

It was the same establishment in which Sir Giles and Tom and Sally were staying. Without the pilgrims who flooded its streets in summer, Sarria was a small town with a choice of hostels and pensions but fewer hotels.

# CHAPTER TWELVE

*Richard joins the team.*

That evening at eight, once they had planned for the next day and after they settled their guests, Richard took Miguel to one side.

"Can we find a coffee before you go home?"

"Of course, this is Spain. There's always a bar around."

"Somewhere private," he said, his expression reflecting his intent.

"Come on, no one will disturb us in the bar round the corner."

It was very Galician, brown and basic. Empty other than a group of elderly men playing cards by the window. With a good, strong café cortado, there was the opportunity to talk. They sat beside the pellet burner, the gentle roar of which would ensure that their conversation was private.

"I can guess what you want to say, but allow me to explain my offer, then I promise I'll let you make up your own mind."

Richard hesitated and then nodded. "Go ahead."

"As you must have gathered, I am the colonel of a special guardia unit which comes under the judiciary rather than the police department. It's partly intelligence gathering and deals with major crime. There are several such units in the country."

Miguel leaned back, and his chair creaked in protest, distracting Richard for a moment. The conversation and Miguel's gaze were intense and protesting of the chair lightened the atmosphere.

"My unit's office is in Madrid, and I have a room in Sarria. We cover Northwest Spain, but we work internationally as a section of the Guardia Civil, which is why we wear the uniform on formal occasions. We are autonomous, which means we use plain clothes and go undercover as needed."

Miguel was watching him, his eyes narrowed, and he was unsure how to react.

"I had gathered most of that." Richard nodded.

"I hand-pick my team and they are very experienced. If you worked with the unit, it would broaden our expertise. The general has discussed it with his British counterpart and agrees. We have cleared it at the ministerial level in both countries. You would keep your old rank and pay, but work as a consultant. I will try to make it permanent, in which case MI6 or Interpol would discuss your employment conditions."

That shocked Richard into silence. Miguel had invited him to be a volunteer, but this would change his life again.

When he escaped from both police work and London, he needed peace and tranquillity to heal, but he missed being a detective. Now he would have to choose.

"Thank you, but I need time to think."

"Of course?"

"You've taken the wind out of my sails... But I would like to move home."

"In that case, may I suggest something...?"

"I can't cope with any more suggestions."

"Practical at this stage. The young couple, Tom and Sally, return to Sheffield in the morning. Help me with their interview tonight, and tomorrow meet my team and we'll talk about what your role would be. Try your desk and see how it feels to be an official part of the investigation."

"You can be quite persuasive."

"The downside is Jane Landis becomes your responsibility."

"Am I no longer a suspect, then?"

"I am pretty sure you are a victim and our murderer placed Molly for you to find. You said you remember nothing of the bombing, but I assume you witnessed a person or a transaction that puts you in danger, or they believe you did."

Richard was quiet. What more was there to say?

"I've scheduled the interview for 9pm, leaving you time for a shower. This identification gives you access to all areas of the barracks."

He held out a badge with the insignia of his team and Richard's name and rank.

Richard's hesitation was only momentary, but he was shaking his head as he took the token, aware that once again Miguel was propelling him out of his comfort zone. The colonel looked relieved, his face clearing.

Once Richard had showered and changed his clothes, he would consider the position he found himself in.

If it was a temporary thing, he could then return to

painting. Recreating beauty, listening to stories the pilgrims told and walking through the mist, knowing sunshine was there just waiting.

He enjoyed the work, and it was a relief to be included, but he had deliberately escaped from that world where part of the job was to look evil in the eye daily.

"Why do you keep an office in Sarria?" Richard asked Miguel.

"Carolina has a law practice here, and my parents live here and their parents before them." He paused, trying to articulate the actual cause.

"Because I need a reason to be human and to be part of a community where finding a lost dog and getting people home from the fiesta is policing. Where I can catch a fish in the river and eat it with vegetables I grew."

Richard shared that sentiment, but was it a fantasy? The problem was that here in this part of Galicia; it was tantalisingly real.

"The new job changes that?"

"Yes, but it doesn't change my desire to feel normal." Miguel said.

When we were operational, I was required to be away. Between times, I consulted for different departments and teams when they called for my expertise. Now I am in charge of the department and everyone who works in it. All decisions will fall to me and the board of Justice."

"Are all the units based in Madrid?"

"No, Eastern Spain has an office in Barcelona, which makes sense as they also cover Spanish terrorism. Catalonia and the Basque country are traditional training grounds."

"So you could base your team here?" he asked.

Miguel seemed surprised at that suggestion, but it fell

like a ripe seed into fertile ground.

# CHAPTER THIRTEEN

## *Roles*

On Tuesday morning, Richard met the chief inspector and her sergeant in the reception at the guardia barracks, but there was no sign of the professor.

"Are we waiting for Lord Southerby?" He asked.

"He'll come when we need him. I was expecting the colonel."

He raised his eyebrows and said nothing else.

"This way then."

He took her a short distance to the conference room, explaining that it was hers as long as needed. She didn't display further disappointment at dealing with him, other than to say,

"I am sorry, Richard. I didn't realise you had official status here, otherwise I would have contacted you before we came."

"It's new to me, only ratified yesterday and agreed this morning."

He smiled at her, ignoring the patronising tone,

wanting to keep the relationship friendly for as long as possible. He was expecting a backlash, a reason why she must work with Miguel.

"Time is not on our side, so will you brief me on your part of the case, or do you need to get organised first?"

"Oh, John will set everything up. Where can we meet in the meantime?"

He only hesitated for a moment.

"Of course, my temporary accommodation is in the barracks, so we can go there."

Jane raised her eyebrows in question, but followed him.

Once in his apartment, Richard made coffee, and they sat at his kitchen table while Jane took in their surroundings.

He explained, knowing it was none of her business.

"The body was hanging on my fence and the incident room occupies my gallery. Miguel thought I was safer here until we find the link."

"Of course, that's the primary reason I came myself. Sir Giles has received death threats against him and his family and we take terrorist activity seriously. Although I can't imagine why you think that you are in danger."

"Because why kill someone in a remote part of Spain rather than choosing a more political target? Also, no one has claimed responsibility. Since Molly and I have links to the museum bombing, isn't that the most likely reason?"

"But this isn't a radical cell operating from a Bradford bedroom. The IRA is a sophisticated multi-national association, working to destabilise the Middle East and create a conduit for weapons into Iran."

Jane stood and gazed out of his window, her back to him. The sneer in her voice jangled his nerves.

"So, why Molly and why here?"

"Sir Giles is part of a group of MP's and business people who got lucrative arms deals with the Saudis, but who refused to sell military supplies to Iran.

"Several of them have received specific death threats suggesting they will target family members first. I have copies of all the letters available."

"Why here?"

"Opportunity, I advised Molly not to come because it's easier to protect her at home. We sent a detective posing as her boyfriend, but he has disappeared, as you already know."

The anger burned, but the chief Inspector was looking at him for a reaction, so he smiled and said.

"That explains why we couldn't find out about him. I wish you had told us sooner."

"Miguel's team has all the paperwork."

"Yes, I'm sure they do, but they needed it last week."

"Classified. Too many important trade deals at stake and if Miguel was informed, so was the Spanish government and we lacked proof of terrorist activity at the time."

"OK, so where is this evidence?" Richard was in control now.

"That's why we brought Professor Bonham. He has material relating to the Iran Russia Alliance."

"Information or proof?"

"He's a duke?" Jane's voice implied a duke was incapable of having none vital intelligence. So he tried again.

"Do you think John is ready? Let's gather all our materials together because the colonel wanted to have a case conference at 12.30."

"Great, I have authority to set up a joint task force to hunt down this organisation and we may need to get America involved. No disrespect, Richard, but this is out of your league. What level of security clearance do you have?"

He didn't know if he had any, so he kept quiet. He had convinced himself that he wanted to be here, but today he doubted it again. Politics was his reason for leaving police work and Jane was now playing a game he despised, casting around for a justification to bypass him.

He decided not to retaliate.

Whilst he was thinking this, Jane was waiting for an answer.

"National security is at stake, also the lives of Britain's most important people. This is not the same as dealing with a domestic on Luton common."

The reference was to one of Richard's well publicised previous cases. A man who's overbearing wife frightened him and so he killed four stay-at-home mums. It wasn't international terrorism, but nor was it 'a domestic'. His hands tightened on the grips of his sticks and he pushed himself to his feet and started toward the door.

"Let's see if John has finished. After that, I'll explain which areas you have access to. There's time before the briefing."

"No, it won't work, because I cannot tell you any more or offer you any confidential documents until I have assurance of your clearance."

"That's fine. Of course, you can remain here if you don't wish to accompany me."

Then nodding in agreement, he very deliberately misunderstood her comment.

"But.... you cannot get back to your conference room without my badge. Sadly, it will take me a while to locate someone with the authorisation..... There is milk in the fridge if you want coffee while you wait."

"Don't be... I meant..."

"In that case, perhaps we can deal with one problem at once."

Richard didn't raise his voice, but it shook him. Naturally, he expected Jane to challenge his authority because he knew from experience how she worked. But was surprised to feel both inadequate and undermined, making petty, spiteful comments in retaliation was so tempting.

The walk back was silent, except for showing his reluctant colleague where she could go and where she needed an escort. This didn't faze her, and he was sure she planned to bypass the process.

The room was ready, and the sergeant had prepared the information that Jane needed.

"Are we meeting Lord Bonham at the briefing?"

"The commander will talk to you when you arrive."

John turned to Richard. "Sir, don't forget the file that you put on that table earlier."

The folio wasn't his, and he had never seen it before today. The sergeant's face was expressionless and gave him no clues, so he picked it up and nodded.

"sergeant."

Miguel was waiting when he showed Jane to the operations centre and then Richard excused himself, slipping into the chair of his new desk. The room smelt of dust, cleaning fluid and bodies and it evoked feelings which were so familiar. He glanced around him, but everyone was busy preparing for the meeting and no one took much notice of him.

They did watch Jane and Miguel, who could clearly be seen arguing, through the office window.

While he waited, he peeked at the file and it looked as though John had copied the information the British police had.

The sergeant put his job on the line in doing so, as it contained the confidential documents that Chief inspector Landis didn't think he had clearance to read. Once again checking his other colleagues to ensure that he wasn't being watched, he slipped the folder into his top drawer and turned the key. After which he moved to the conference table that filled the centre, taking a notepad and pencil. Ana handed them headphones for simultaneous translation and reminded them to bear that in mind when speaking.

Miguel publicly welcomed Jane and gave her the floor. She clarified she was wasting her time without Lord Bonham being here to report. There was a shuffling and Manuel stood and passed out papers, the professor's statement and statements from the Westminster bombers confessing to their Muslim links, and correspondence between members of the IRA. He looked at the DCI and said,

"I hope that these will help, chief inspector."

Jane talked through the British investigation into the death threats, the information they had on the Iran Russia Alliance, and the suggestion that it was time to involve the American intelligence agencies. He listened to the team's questions and felt they were over thinking this, sure that they had missed something simple.

The meeting concluded with the domestic investigation being closed. He would have his gallery back if the incident room was no longer needed. Then they could debrief Sir Giles and arrange a date to have Molly's body taken home and the private investigator could leave.

The inquiry had both become smaller and more far-reaching and complex. They began with secure communication systems for dealing with other agencies. No problem, as they had set up the basics for Miguel to use.

Richard was focused on the file he was given. When John Hollis had worked for him, he never came close to breaking a rule. He didn't take risks or use his initiative, so this file must contain important documents to cause him to act out of character.

# CHAPTER FOURTEEN

## *More information*

Later that evening, the second interview with Molly's friends hinted at a lead. Sally remembered the name of the group leader of the organisation that Molly was part of. It was Michael Boolson. He had a girlfriend, and she didn't know her name or any more details.

She wondered if the couple they had dinner with were Michael and his girlfriend. Sally didn't recognise him, but they knew Molly from university. With someone following Molly before she died and the police asking so many questions, it made her think.

The next morning, Richard met Miguel's team, and they welcomed him with open arms. No one questioned his inclusion, either openly or marked by hesitation or lack of eye contact. He asked Miguel why he didn't need to fight for respect.

"We function as a paramilitary army unit, so we accept orders and our cases are dangerous, so petty resentments put someone's life in danger. We all are aware of that. Also, we have special times to iron out disputes, we go away for the weekend and consider the change or new member, any doubts, dislikes, minor or major problems with the current arrangement. I cannot make your contract permanent before that's happened, and your acceptance has to be unanimous. We all know that and it protects you, giving you a chance to settle in and defends the sense of unity the team has."

"Ah, so I'm on trial."

"No, for this operation, you are one of us. We'll consider the future later."

"And you?"

"Oh, my mind's made up already."

Richards' primary responsibility was to liaise with the British police. He suspected that Jane Landis wasn't pleased, but he was the obvious candidate. Miguel decided that time was against them, so they gave the professor to someone else to handle, with a newly appointed translator to help. The entire unit spoke basic English, but Ana was fluent and wouldn't miss details. They sent Sergeant Elvira Gómez from the guardia to interview Sir Giles once again. The colonel introduced them and asked more questions about Jack, the threatening letters, and Molly's friend. The officer planned to act as victim liaison until he could return Molly home, replacing Ana, who they now required to interpret. The team sifted through the mountains of information and intelligence. The problem was finding what they lacked and recognising its importance. Richard listened with fascination as they discussed administrative details of the job and what needed to change, another project that was outside of his experience.

This affair was stretching the infrastructure to the breaking point, filling the spare offices in the barracks. There wasn't enough equipment to go round, including phone lines.

Expense claims and overtime had been approved. And officers found from nearby garrisons, and local police to help.

Manuel told him that the café closest to the headquarters had doubled its turnover in the last few days.

Now the team planned to focus on the terrorists, which required fewer staff members but more technology. But finding information on the so-called IRA was proving difficult and the only material they had came from the professor.

As for local leads, Jack had vanished, and they couldn't locate either the lady in green or the friendly couple who still didn't have names other than Mike and Jane, with no surname, so Michael Boolson was at least a place to start.

On Thursday morning, Richard volunteered to drive the private investigator employed by Sir Giles to the airport, so missing the next meeting. The previous day's session had frustrated him because putting their resources into the IRA was losing their momentum. The detective might have ideas to help him make sense of it and suggest a different approach to the team.

People often gave information in informal chats, and he wasn't looking for evidence. He wanted clues to things they might have missed. In his opinion, the investigator was being allowed home before his evidence was analysed. The man was trained to observe, so he must have noticed something. The focus of terrorism put them in danger of missing the obvious.

Sir Giles's assistant rang that morning as there was paperwork her boss wanted to talk about. He agreed to collect the file and arrange a time later in the day.

The investigator was staying at a nearby pension, so he suggested they meet in the hotel lobby when he collected the file. She handed over the folder and suggested he and Sir Giles have coffee at five that afternoon. As she turned to leave, the private detective walked across the lobby. Richard hesitated, thinking he was a pilgrim, wanting direction, but of course, he dressed as a walker, because he had to be invisible while following Molly. He was still speculating when the guy held out his hand.

"Dave Bromley. You must be the chief inspector."

"Richard Harris, so just Richard these days. I forgot I was looking for a pilgrim."

"Shame I never got to finish because I enjoyed that part. Who were you talking to?"

"Geraldine, the assistant to Sir Giles, but surely you have met her before. Wasn't she the one who hired you?"

"Everything by phone and email and reported via a message service." Dave fixed his eyes on the stairs, even after she had disappeared.

"Is something wrong?"

"Yes. No, no. Nothing." The man shook his head in denial.

"OK. I guess we'd better go then. The car is this way."

He wondered whether to push the detective to tell him what had bothered him.

"So, you have ruled out the locals and her friends as suspects?" said the private eye.

"Who told you that?"

"I am leaving without an interview. That says hit man to me," he said.

Richard laughed, taking the sting from his next question.

"Is second guessing the investigation a speciality?"

"All part of the job, well maybe not now, since I'm paid up to date, and I failed to protect her. Mind you, her boyfriend was a police officer, and he's vanished. At least I'm still here."

"How did you discover he was undercover?"

"Oh, I heard them talking about it. And although Molly had a certain charm, I try not to get involved with my clients."

He sat up straighter. If Molly knew that Jack was the police, it changed things.

"Also, the other chief inspector phoned to say I was no longer needed, and she mentioned it then." Richard wondered why Jane had mentioned it, but the man was still talking. "Good job too, as it was costing me to stay."

He looked at him quizzically.

"Well,... OK, so I inflated the bill a bit to cover emergencies."

"I'll not judge. We all need to earn a living."

He hoped Dave might talk on the way since he was a mine of information.

Dave described his time in Galicia. And Richard liked his self-effacing humour. And when he didn't claim they did the same job, Richards' respect increased.

He left his details.

"When dirty work needs to be done. One other thing, Geraldine, that assistant, looks identical to the woman in the green coat. I can't swear to it because I only saw her in hiking gear, but she is the same height and build."

Richard put the business card in his pocket, smiling as he walked away from the departure lounge. Guys such as this reminded him of London, his old job, and familiar territory.

On his return, he went back into an uncomfortable political minefield. He was way out of his league Jane had been right about that.

# CHAPTER FIFTEEN

## *Gregory Bonham*

At that moment, Professor Gregory Bonham (The Duke of Southerby) was unhappy. Jane persuaded him that flying on that damnable Irish aeroplane was helping their cause, and now he found himself in an inadequate hotel, in a dingy town in the middle of nowhere. He had assumed they would invite him to meetings, but so far that hadn't happened and he was bored.

He left his 'man' at home and he was wearing despicable clothing and he wished he hadn't listened to her. He was there to convince anyone listening that Muslims were terrorists and that Middle Eastern Nations needed subduing if the superior western nations were to gain back their sovereignty.

The gods gifted him with intelligence and genetic superiority and it was his task to restore power to those ordained to use it. Gregory believed there were more important things to do than watch farms and many of his class were reduced to that.

Gregory Bonham liked power even more than he liked money. He called himself a patriot and felt Britain was in grave danger of losing its national identity and it was the responsibility of people such as himself to restore that national pride. The group he formed for this purpose was growing. Public opinion was changing, and soon the time would be right for genuine leaders.

Jane told him to adopt the role of absent-minded professor because the Spanish police needed to concentrate on his ability, not his rank. She had explained this standing naked in his London apartment. He agreed whilst they were sipping champagne in his hot tub, thinking about the enticing way her breasts moved in response to the swirling water. Now he regretted his weakness.

It was a tiresome few days. The local police interviewed him as though he were a suspect in this case and neither understood his role nor his importance. What should he have expected from them? The more he thought, the more he wondered whether playing politics worked and if action was more effective. If one death had got him here, maybe more deaths would achieve their goals.

At least Jane was alluring, and he admitted she was useful.


On Friday morning, Miguel and Manuel invited Richard to watch the interview with Professor Bonham.

'Or should they call him Lord? His clothes were stereotypical of an untidy and absent-minded university academic, but he was, in fact, a Duke. He cast his mind back to his own research.

Lord Gregory Bonham had been the Duke of Southerby for ten years. His younger brother managed the estate and lived in the west wing of Southerby Hall. The main house was open to the public, and Gregory and his mother kept small apartments in the east wing. The arrangement suited them, as they had opened the house and gardens to the population at large to make the building's maintenance workable. His biography said that in order to give time to his academic work, he spent most of his time in his London apartment or working in university archives researching parliamentary history.

Something in his bearing betrayed a sharp mind, but his clothes were too stereotypical.

He described the tension in the Middle East, the hostility between Iran and Saudi Arabia. The explanation was technical, but he summed it up as follows.

"Britain has close ties to Saudi Arabia and sells arms. Iran wants to buy Arms. Britain won't sell to Iran. Russia will."

"So what is the IRA?" Manuel asked.

"It is a group wanting to use Russia as a conduit for arms into Iran."

"Why would they threaten people?"

"To stop us from selling our armaments to Saudi Arabia."

"And then what happens?"

"Then Muslim groups in Iran attack the west, of course."

"The attempted bombing?"

"Some radical Muslims won't wait, hence terrorist attacks, but mark my words, this is a war, Islam against all civilised countries."

Then, he produced correspondence with prominent business people, supporting his theory.

The men turned to Richard.

"What do you think?"

"Something seems off."

"His evidence convinced your friend, Chief Inspector Landis, and our contact in the CIA."

"And you two?".

"On the surface everything looks OK, but his answers seemed rehearsed and his explanation for Saudi, Iran relations very simplistic, nothing I could explain to the CIA,".

"Let me guess, they are pulling rank."

Richard's face showed a smile, but his heart was sinking. The USA, with Britain's help, had invaded Iraq without concrete evidence recently. If this became explosive, would it be necessary to invade Iran?

"We need to slow down. To understand why the professor is here, we should pay more attention to him. Richard, you take him for coffee as soon as you get a chance and have a friendly chat, Manuel. You inquire into his background. I'll call in a few favours."

"Is Jane still insisting that he come to briefings?"

"Yes, she is, and it won't happen and our doubts remain unofficial and between us for the moment," said Miguel.

Chus, another member of Miguel's team, interrupted them at that point. She had found a significant link between prominent business people and the IRA that needed attention.

Talking to the professor was the best use of his time, so he phoned to suggest they meet for a drink.

"Official or unofficial?" The professor asked.

"Informal, but I'm happy to answer any questions you have."

There was an edge to the tone. "I hoped you would ask some questions."

"Yes, I might have queries, but personal, not official. Can you find Cafe Central in half an hour?"

The concerns for Richard's safety faded as the investigation progressed. He was living in the barracks. Going out didn't trouble him, he didn't even think about it?

# CHAPTER SIXTEEN

## *What's in a title?*

The professor was there when Richard walked into the busy café. It was a sunny afternoon, so customers packed the outside tables around the patio heaters. But Gregory Bonham was at a table inside under the television.

As he adjusted to the light, he studied the man. The professor wore a faded jacket with patched pockets and a rumpled shirt, half-moon glasses in front of him. With a stiff, military posture, he drummed his fingers on the polished wood in front of him. The minute he spotted Richard, his shoulders slumped, and he adopted the vague expression he had used earlier.

Lord Bonham was acting, but why? Although, after his conversation with Miguel and Manuel, he expected it. A series of impressions fleeted across Richard's mind. The professor looked academic. In fact, the image of someone who spends hours in dusty archives. He overdid it though, a stereotype, not reality.

The professor chose the table so that no one could

overhear because the music was loud enough to cover the sound of conversation. Now it was time for some acting of his own.

"Thank you for coming here. Very generous when you must be busy."

"The English detectives believe my opinion is important, but Spanish police have been sceptical."

The emphasis was on the word English.

"No, not at all. What you say is remarkable, and the statements you gave caused a great deal of interest."

With effort, he sounded enthusiastic, not sarcastic.

"I didn't realise you knew so much about parliamentary history and I spent this morning with the colonel telling him about your exhibition."

Neither of them were talented actors, so for Richard, the overwhelming wish was to laugh. To help control his reaction, he gripped his coffee cup as he glanced at the professor, expecting to see amusement, but the man was nodding in appreciation.

"Hasn't your Westminster exhibition gone on tour?" Richard asked.

Now sober, because the Duke didn't query his flattery. In fact, he drank it in, becoming more voluble with each compliment. It was a tactic to remember.

"Yes, two years, having started with a nationwide tour. It's very popular and I am proud of what my small presentation has achieved. What's your role here? I understood you had retired?"

The forgetful professor's act was slipping. The arrogance of someone brought up knowing that his family was only one step from royalty was showing. He was fidgeting in his seat, as if distancing himself from the surrounding people. He showed a moment's distaste whilst sipping his coffee, as though the cup were substandard. Maybe this café was too ordinary.

"I have retired. In fact, I have become an artist. We found Molly outside my gallery and they have co-opted me in for this investigation because of the individuals involved. I have a grasp of British culture the Spanish police lack, as you have noticed."

Richard's tone of voice mollified him. He continued, keeping his tone respectful.

"Jane reminded the team here that you are a duke, so should I address you as '*Your Grace*'."

"Professor, or your grace, either is acceptable. Lord Bonham is incorrect. On this trip I wanted to emphasis my qualifications, not my status, so Professor or Dr Bonham would be best."

"Of course, that's why I asked. I suspected you would have a professional reason for using your academic title, rather than emphasising your rank. We have now made the officers aware of your status."

"Indeed, indeed, few men of my rank have a doctorate, or bother with universities. Not sure the Spanish understand our aristocracy. I thought it better to reassure them I have qualifications." He paused and his expression changed, as though needing time to arrange the features.

"Sorry about your wife, by the way... damned shame, damned shame. These Arabs will stop at nothing, no morals."

"They were both from Birmingham with British parents, I was told." The statement puzzled Richard, having never blamed Gill's death on race or religion.

"I insisted on English waiting staff, so I hadn't expected them to send Arabs or Muslims."

Richard raised his eyebrows, surprised the professor

had broken the law on racism with such nonchalance.

"Of course, they were posing as servers?" said Richard.

"Don't you recall?"

"No. I remember the sound of the bomb and not much else."

"So, what do you remember?" The question was abrupt.

He closed his eyes. The query disturbed him, but he answered.

"I recall arriving with my wife, being informed that we had a half hour before the exhibition closed. They were about to set up for your reception. I have a gap in my memory after that. I think I heard Gill screaming my name, then I woke up in the hospital and that's all."

Relief and delight showed on the professor's face, but he masked it with such speed that Richard wasn't sure he'd seen it. When Richard's eyes opened fully, he only saw concern.

"How terrible, just dreadful, and you'll never realise what you achieved? You were quite a hero, you know."

"My wife died that night. The doctors thought I would remember, but I don't wish to. I want Gill to be..."

The professor patted his arm. "Terrible, terrible," he was saying.

The conversation after that was stilted. The mention of his spouse still shook him, and he had an overwhelming desire to go home. He took a deep breath.

"I'm sure they will ask you to become more involved after today, if you would like to?"

"Oh Yes, that's why I came. I'm positive the local boys mean well... We are here now bringing our expertise.... and I understand the Americans are joining us so the police here can get back to finding stolen tractors or whatever they do."

Everything was going through Richard's mind. The professor wants to influence the investigation and for that; he needs Jane Landis in charge.

He assumed that laws or morals of society didn't apply to him.

The acting puzzled him, although he didn't question his ability he doubted that a middle eastern terrorist organisation was involved?

Richard decided not to go straight to the barracks. Although the shadows were lengthening, he had over two hours before he lost the light, so instead, he walked along the riverbank until he had left the town behind, relaxing as he strolled.

Despite the shortness of the spring day, the sunlight warmed his back. Only the depth of the shadow under the trees betrayed the approaching evening. The clean air helped mosses thrive on the old walls and tree branches. Leaves were still vibrant and tentative, and the sun's rays had plenty of room between the emerging greenery for its shimmering descent. Wild flowers were breaking through the winter leaves and primrose, wild strawberry and violets provided splashes of colour to the path's edge. He was glad of the quiet. Another month and his solitude would have been less certain. He passed a couple of hopeful anglers and a jogger, but no one else. He couldn't help thinking of the night of the bombing. What if he knew something? What if Molly's murder was a warning to him and to Sir Giles? If he could remember, he might find the key.

Even as he pondered, he noticed someone coming behind him, sprinting. He tried to move out of the way and his leg, unstable and unable to recover from sudden movement, tipped him into the river.

It was his injured limb that saved him. As he fell, a sharp pain shot through his side, then his mouth filled with water and he attempted to right himself. The splash attracted an angler on the riverbank to help.

He saw a hooded figure running off along the path, but the light was fading and they appeared only as a dark shape. A fisherman, on a small wooden jetty, grasped his hand and pulled, and he stood in the waist-deep river. He stopped, shocked, then scrambled up the bank with his new friend's help. Once on the path, he shivered, his whole body shaking, and the last of the sun left with the speed of his attacker.

'Was he attacked?' He asked himself, 'or had a thoughtless runner bumped into him causing him to fall?' There was a wooden seat, onto which he sank, not sure that he could walk despite the angler's encouragement.

His rescuer wore waders, but the water was deep and freezing, and the air was getting colder as the sun dropped behind the trees. He became aware the stranger was talking to him, telling him they must move and something to do with his car.

Richard struggled to his feet, and they began a slow limping procession. The angler had to support him because his injured leg was so painful and he had lost his stick. They made it to where a steep route led upwards through the trees, away from the main path. The man helped him to a fallen log and disappeared.

He jumped at every sound because it was dark where he sat, and he was freezing and feeling faint. He hadn't understood the last thing he was told before the guy disappeared. The river had soaked both his phone and his watch. Just as he realised the danger he was in, the man returned with a blanket in his arms and helped him to take off his wet jacket to wrap the cover round him.

The angler pointed to Richard's side, and he saw blood. It had soaked his shirt and the blanket and when he moved his clothes, he was bleeding from a deep gash, but he was woozy now and tried to pull the blanket round him. His friend stopped what he was doing and pressed something to the wound, telling him to hold it there.

By then, Richard was losing consciousness and his surroundings were becoming more a dream than reality. Despite remaining upright, he was swaying like a reed in the wind.

Before he knew what was happening, a paramedic had helped him into an ambulance. By the time they reached the medical centre, he was warmer, more alert, and embarrassed. He needed stitches, and his leg was going to be painful for days.

There were voices before a nurse ushered in Miguel and the doctor. They were discussing him.

"He will need to rest, at least until the injury heals and we remove the stitches. He was lucky that he fell into the water and the cold slowed the blood flow. Had it been warmer, he would have bled out.

"Was it a knife wound?"

"Oh, undoubtedly. The blade used was a very narrow 15 to 20 cm long, hard to tell because the fall forced the blade to one side. You had a fortuitous break because it interrupted the thrust, reducing the force."

Miguel and the doctor were acting out the scenarios. They knew each other.

"No, it was a jogger, and I tried to move, but the path was wet and my injured leg gave way, so I fell into the water, cutting myself on the bank."

"Oh, but we have a witness, and we have confirmed the knife wound, so you are lucky to be alive, my friend."

Richard was only wearing a paper gown, and it embarrassed him: he felt outnumbered and angry because no one treated him seriously? The doctor collected trousers and a sweater for him from a charity bin so that Miguel could drive him to the barracks. But he was in pain and daren't think what his appearance was like.

He wished he was sure it was an accident. Only this morning, he had convinced himself that there was no real danger and now things had changed and being involved in complex international crime made him want to run.

At the moment, he wanted to paint pictures and be a mild-mannered English watercolour artist. Anything but this.

Then he remembered he should meet Sir Giles in five minutes' time, and it jolted him out of his self-pity. What should he do? He needed a story, a reason to postpone the meeting. Do they treat it as nothing or dramatise the event?

"Down play everything if you are willing, because it is more dangerous for you."

"How so?"

"If you say you fell, they might try again, but we could be ready next time."

"The group have been unlucky so far."

"But they think you know something important."

"About this murder?"

"Or the bombing or the connection between them?"

"Trouble is, I don't," said Richard, his frustration making him snap "OK, let me phone Sir Giles. I'll say I fell in the river and will see him tomorrow morning."

Miguel took him to the barracks for clothes before taking him home that night. When Richard protested,

Miguel insisted they need to talk in private, persuading Richard to lie on the back seat until they were out of town, which was overkill or another one of Miguel's jokes.

"I have bad news," he said as they were getting out of the car.

"Oh?"

"Someone broke into your house while you were with the doctor and I'm uncertain if anything is missing."

"No worries, I'll check in the morning after I've talked to Sir Giles."

"No. We are here to talk about what to do next."

Carolina came and hustled them into the warm kitchen with her parents and the children. Everything was ready with the table set for dinner. The meal was very Galician, with plentiful, hot country food. Hot soup, mountains of potatoes and grilled meat, and a salad from the garden, with cheese cake for dessert. Richard had eaten only snack food that day. A home cooked supper amid this lively welcoming family tasted wonderful, but even as he watched these lovely smiling faces, he knew he might put them at risk.

Galicia never appeared dangerous, not in the way London sometimes does. Early morning walks or strolling back from a restaurant along his dark secluded lane never felt risky. In fact, danger had never crossed his mind. Beyond locking the door, he didn't think of a burglary. And now, in this kitchen, it seemed impossible he was at risk.

The men retired to Miguel's study after dinner. Richard wanted to help, although Carolina, a lawyer, explained to him that when she had an important case in court, roles were reversed. So Carolina and her parents cleared up and sorted out the children.

"What is your opinion of the Duke of Sutherland?

Manuel has found some significant things, but I'd like your impressions first."

Richard voiced his thoughts. "He is acting the role of a professor and he is not absent minded nor vague but wants us to think he is... He is both a racist and a misogynist, neither of which he tries to hide. Besides that, his reason for not using his title doesn't work. In Britain, we mutter about the aristocracy but a duke can open most doors." Miguel was nodding.

"So you don't like him much?"

"Oh, I've met plenty of his type and none of the things I mentioned make him a murderer."

"What if I told you he was once part of a nationalist, fascist group and the Sheffield police arrested him for inciting hatred likely to cause a riot?"

Richard nodded. "Of course, I remember now... that explains everything."

"It does?"

"Absolutely. His record is on file, although it was a few years ago, and his arrest was a very public affair. '*Lord Bonham arrested with thugs,*' the headline read. His family concealed the details and needed both money and influence to keep things quiet. As you would imagine, there was a talented lawyer who got him a suspended sentence whilst his fellow conspirators went to gaol." Richard took a sip of his brandy and settled in to his tale.

"Of course, I met him the museum, but even then he looked familiar. If I remember correctly, the rumour was that his parents kept him on a short leash and he disappeared from public view. When his father died, and he inherited the title of duke, he announced he planned to concentrate on his academic work and would not stand for election to the House of Lords and handed over the running of the estate to his younger brother."

Richard paused. "This information makes him less suspicious because he doesn't want to remind people he is a fascist with a criminal conviction."

Miguel had listened with interest.

"Yes, I am inclined to agree on both counts. There is a solid reason for his odd behaviour and it might explain why he assumes he should be part of the investigation. In his normal life, he can take his entitlement for granted."

The men chatted for an hour before joining Carolina and her parents for a late brandy. Richard deciding that he loved this family and home and understood why Miguel didn't want to sacrifice that.

# CHAPTER SEVENTEEN

## *Realisation*

When he arrived at Sir Giles's hotel the next morning, Geraldine and the professor were deep in conversation in the lobby. In fact, they looked as though they were arguing. They jumped apart as Richard approached.

"It's good to catch up with you, Gregory," she said, her voice loud in the quiet lobby. She turned to Richard. "Sir Giles helped with sponsorship for the Westminster Exhibition. I took care of the administration."

Richard said, "I am surprised that you required sponsorship, professor."

"Oh, it's about more than money, dear boy. We needed names, politicians, and business people. The money buys better ways to exhibit, but the contacts get us better places."

He turned to Geraldine, "I must rush, I'm meeting Jane."

"Sir Giles is in his sitting area, if you follow me."

Sir Giles was in the hotel's penthouse suite and she

ushered Richard into a compact but well appointed sitting room. He ordered coffee and inquired how Richard was after his accident whilst they waited.

"Quite embarrassed," said Richard.

"It forced nearby anglers to pull me out of the river."

"How is your side?"

"My side?"

"I understood a ruffian attacked you,"

"Gosh no, my leg gave way on the wet ground and I lost my stick in the river. I was certain I'd be there all night and freezing cold by the time someone arrived. The doctor checked for hypothermia and a glass of brandy and a warm fire cured my pride."

"I must have misunderstood, but I'm glad that you have recovered now."

"I'm keeping away from rough ground and rivers for a while."

Richard moved to ease the pressure on his leg.

"I'm afraid of damaging my hip again. The doctor reminded me that any further damage would put me in a wheelchair."

"Do you recall the bombing at all? I appreciate what you did in the museum, but I wish it was me and not Molly this time around."

"Not much."

"Do you expect to remember more?" Geraldine asked.

"The specialist told me I had an emotional block called *psychogenic amnesia*. In theory, my memory will return in the future.

"Perhaps he doesn't want to relive the details, Geraldine," said Sir Giles with uncharacteristic thoughtfulness.

"It might be helpful if it links the two cases," she

responded.

"It would be, but I can't get past hearing my wife's scream."

The coffee arrived, preventing any more conversation. As soon as they poured it, Richard answered their questions on the case and thanked Sir Giles for hunting out the paperwork about the threats on his life and his correspondence from the IRA. He assured the minister that they were sure to have something concrete soon.

"You need to discover why, not only who killed Molly. We must stop them before someone else's daughter..." he could not finish.

Richard gave him the time he needed to recover. This side of the man was nicer than he had seen before.

"I'm leaving now that I can take my daughter home. Is there a reason to stay?"

"No. We are happy to keep you informed at home if you would like. Perhaps you could give me contact numbers and your schedule so we can find you should anything come up."

"I've booked Sir Giles a flight for this afternoon, so I'll take him to the airport, come back for Molly's things and fly back myself later."

A guardia interrupted them again with a message for Richard, so he made his apologies and left with the officer. Miguel prearranged the interrupter, because Richard's life was in danger and assigned someone to go with him to appointments. Richard didn't like it when the colonel mentioned it, but when he awoke that morning, his leg and side were stiff and painful and he was glad not to drive. It took self-control to walk to Sir Giles' suite without showing his pain.

He swallowed more painkillers in the car as he was

keen to make the twelve thirty briefing today and the meeting was going to be lengthy. They had by now collected mountains of information, including suspects, but nothing concrete to link them. No terrorist group, including the IRA, had claimed responsibility, which was unusual, so they were overdue for an in-depth review.

The review didn't happen that day. Richard was told when he returned that anglers had discovered the body of Jack Clarke and Police Divers had pulled him out of the reservoir at Portomarin.

He phoned Miguel, who was at the scene.

"Who found him?"

"Kids in a canoe spotted a rucksack and told the fisherman nearby. He thought it best to call us and not touch anything. Divers have found him, so I'll let you know when we get back."

Jack Clarke was an undercover police officer, working on the death threats, or that's what Jane Landis explained to them. But MPs receive threatening letters or calls every day, especially with the advent of social media. Finding the resources to allocate a detective to each family member was impossible. So what was he working on?

Why was the chief inspector there?

None of it added up in Richard's mind. If Jane Landis came to find Jack Clarke, was he on a secret mission?

Inspector Landis had not been forthcoming and hadn't told them from the beginning that Jack was a police officer, nor why she assigned him to Molly and not Sir Giles unless Molly had been the real target.

He guessed Jane had gone to Portomarin as her office was empty. As he turned to leave, he remembered John Hollis gave him the case file without her knowing.

'Why did he do that when it meant risking his job and his pension?

Something about himself must be important, so he headed to his room to read the folder page by page, word by word.

First, get an update and report. Only Manuel and Chus were there because the others went to Portomarín.

A list of IRA members was being checked, but it didn't look political. The more checking they did, the less criminal activity they found. Although many members were Muslim, they could link none to radical branches and a good half claimed to be Russian orthodox, Catholic, Jewish or non religious. The headed note paper used the initials RIBA, causing doubt whether it was the same organisation.

He told them he would be in his apartment reading paperwork and they agreed to phone with any developments.

So he poured himself a glass of whisky and sat with the information. He felt so much pain that the effects of the alcohol/painkiller combination were welcome. After that, he organised the file on the table and realised that there were two memory sticks: one in a folder marked London Museum and the other IRA Death Threats. There were photos, reports and photocopies of evidence tags. He did the IRA stuff first, as if it were a jigsaw puzzle. After a couple of hours, he found nothing he hadn't expected.

He made instant soup, then, needing to stretch his legs, walked to the front desk to see if they knew what happened at his house. An officer handed him photos of the scene and assured him that they had boarded his door.

He leaned on the counter and ripped open the envelope. He was relieved that the studio was untouched. Paintings weren't worth much in monetary terms, but they represented months of work. The thieves were looking for files. There were papers over the floor, drawers pulled out, and shelves emptied.

"They normally want cash or maybe documents, sir," said the officer.

"I don't keep money in the house, and my documents are here."

It was impossible to look without feeling violated because they had breached the castle he had built since Gill died.

"Perhaps it's people thinking you take payment for the paintings."

That was one possibility, local kids assuming he had a cash box somewhere.

As he returned to his room, he felt broken beyond description and he planned to do something that would cause more pain..

Opening the envelope relating to the London Museum was so hard, but it was time he faced the truth.

Normally, he was not a coward, at least not when confronted with physical danger. Police bravery medals proved that he had rushed in without thinking to apprehend the bombers. But then, if risking your own life makes you a hero. What does rushing in and getting your wife killed make you? That was the question he lived with.

Next, he poured another glass of whisky and, as he sipped, he felt the edges of his world soften. Then he tipped the contents on the table and fired up his laptop and plugged in the memory stick. The texts might match the hard copies, but he needed to know. Even softened by alcohol, the pictures had an effect.

Gill on the ground, a bloody circle round a ragged hole in her dress. They had taken the photos from every angle and they paralysed him.

The pain of seeing her was as bad as he had imagined. He drew deep breaths, tears running down his cheeks, closed his eyes, took one long breath and sat up straight. Before wiping his eyes and forcing himself to continue.

Everything needed a fresh look, so he lay the prints out, using the table extension to make room. And then he sorted the reports into a logical sequence. The comforting familiarity worked with the whisky to take the edge off his pain, physical and mental.

The first time he did this, he was newly promoted to detective sergeant. His role was getting the evidence into order and chasing all the paperwork, a thankless task earning abuse from colleagues, so the new guy got the job. Although referred to as a file, there were boxes and boxes of reports, photographs and tags. Many more than in recent years when technology replaced paper.

Meticulous by nature, he stayed late one evening to organise the crates, intending to get everything into order so that he would know what was missing. He laid it all out and became fascinated, taking most of the night. He had new leads after he re-organised the boxes, but the reception he got from his DI was not encouraging.

His dislike of coarse jokes, swearing, and racist and sexist comments already marked him out as odd, but now he also gained the reputation for being fastidious. But he picked up a taste for detective work and craved success.

By the time he was an inspector, managing evidence was his job.

Many inspectors farmed out as much as possible, but he liked the routine of laying everything out late into the night, making notes and keeping his own catalogue. He made spreadsheets as more were computerised. The spreadsheets developed into the butt of jokes but no one could deny their effectiveness, and his team realised the practise gave them an edge.

As it did years ago, a picture emerged of what had happened in the London Museum, and it disturbed him. Richard didn't attend the trial and couldn't recall the details. He thought he knew the story, but he'd never checked the facts.

When he thought about it, he remembered the Chief Constable's speech had included a brief sequence of the events and description of Richard's actions. Friends gave him snippets of information in the hospital. A trial convicted the bombers of his wife's murder. These fragments had created a narrative. But the photos and the witness statements, together with the floor plan, made it obvious his version was wrong. In fact, it was impossible.

# CHAPTER EIGHTEEN

## *Jack Clarke*

The phone startled Richard. Miguel wanted him at a meeting to discuss the implications of finding Jack's body in half an hour. Richard realised he needed to eat to soak up his three glasses of whisky. He had expected nothing to happen until Monday, as it would take time to piece together what happened to Jack Clark.

An instant coffee, a sandwich and a wash later, he felt human but still aware of the alcohol. He collected a stick and made his way across the barracks. Everyone else had gathered, and Jane glared at him as though he disrupted something of hers.

"Oh, I assumed you'd changed your mind."

Richard said nothing, but sat in an available chair.

Miguel led the briefing, describing the manner in which they found the body, and the probable cause of death.

"A long thin knife and wound to the heart, very similar to Molly Hamilton. The divers discovered a packet of waterlogged documents in the rucksack, but no ID."

"I'm working on it. Don't expect miracles, but I am pretty good."

Everyone laughed and Chus bowed in response

"Sir Giles told us that Jack had a tattoo of a dragon on his forearm, which has given us a temporary ID," said Jane, disapproving of the levity.

"Isn't he flying home?" said Richard.

"Yes, but I phoned him because we couldn't wait for the DNA. The body was intact. And we have photos, but this gives certainty. Meaning that we can assume we have found Jack."

"Although we can't be certain where they killed him, and it looks like the same killer," said Miguel.

"Are we assuming this is a terrorist act? I ask because no one has claimed responsibility, and besides, they go for big impact kills." Raoul asked.

"There is news about that. The victims have received additional threats, and I have copies here." Jane handed copies to everyone.

"So a warning, then?"

Richard didn't see who spoke.

"The group knew he was police because they call him Jack Dawson, his actual name."

"Who else was aware that there was an undercover officer?"

"His chief inspector, and inspector, the rest of my team, the Super, our MI6 contact."

"Not on your unit, then?"

"No one in my line-up fitted the brief. In fact, I'd never met him," said Jane.

"We loaned him from Sheffield, and Inspector Davidson on my team briefed him."

"How many people knew about it?"

"No one outside the job," said Jane.

Richard didn't bother to speak. It sounded as though half of London knew. Miguel interrupted.

"Next, we need to check details, forensics, and how he got to Portomarín."

Richard still wondered why the chief inspector was baiting him because he didn't pose a threat and couldn't hurt or hinder her career, and Miguel gave her the floor in meetings whenever she wanted it.

She resented working with him and not directly with Miguel, so maybe she thought it was his decision not to let the professor into daily briefings. The professor was in Jane's office everyday so she kept him well informed.

Richard listened, and learnt details and team roles, and he settled down, putting his annoyance aside, and watched Miguel.

While Jane worked hard to keep control and authority, Miguel held everyone's attention without effort.

Richard sympathised with her because women needed to work harder for promotion and respect, even in these days of equality.

But the chief inspector chose a route that he despised. Flattering and socialising with her superiors. She ridiculed her team for the smallest mistake and claimed credit for their achievement.

For him, you gained respect by working, listening to people and never cutting corners. He said nothing, but worked harder if anyone challenged his methods.

Miguel was a natural leader and his rapid rise through the ranks showed that. He was still a young man, but his authority was unquestioned. There was a healthy level of banter, but they followed his orders without doubts.

Richard looked round the busy room as everyone was present.

Chus, their forensics expert, Manuel, was a psychologist. Jesús was communications and computer whizz kid. Pedro was a doctor and a pathologist. There was another woman, Carmen, technical support, on maternity leave and the only senior member younger than Miguel.

Miguel had asked Elvira, the guardia sergeant, to lead an administration team, which included John Hollis, and offered extra training and promotion to Ana, the interpreter.

The colonel was talking, going over the forensic details found in Jack's body. The killer cleaned up. They carried out enquiries, but the town was full of pilgrims and no one had noticed him. Still, someone might remember him. So, they rescheduled the case review for Monday evening. To analyse the threatening letters given out by Jane.

# CHAPTER NINETEEN

## *Links to the bombing*

Richard returned to the paperwork. If he treated it like a giant jigsaw puzzle, the more pieces that he fit into place, the easier it would be to find missing evidence. Everything was ready, so he started on a time-line, putting the evidence in order, hoping to remember something.

If he could speak to Gill, ask her what happened, he could apologise, then find out who had done this for her sake.

The first problem he ran into was the timetable itself in which he discovered the bombers couldn't have killed his wife, and yet they were in prison. If he talked to the person in charge, he might discover why, so he searched to see who signed everything. Jane Landis. 'Ah! interesting', but he wasn't ready to question Jane yet.

The next question was how the CPS missed such a crucial piece of material? Why didn't the defence lawyer pick it up either? The bomb makers were being arrested when Gill died, giving them an alibi. Because of that, he needed the material the CPS had used for court. John Hollis was his only hope for quick information, though he wondered if he could call in favours in London if it came to that. He must speak to sergeant Hollis alone, but his leg was too painful for a journey across the barracks. And it was late, so they might have left. He would wait for tomorrow, and so he read the witness testimonies instead.

The other thing that puzzled him was the conflicting reports regarding the detonator. One report suggested he was holding it, another that it was on the chair beside him. Why had it blown up his leg but not his hand or arm? The bomb squad statements answered this. They had found two unfinished bombs, ready for someone to assemble once they were in position. Richard and the officer in charge were talking when they heard the scream. Instinctively, he thrust the device into his pocket and ran, activating a third explosive as he reached the doorway. The door jamb took the blast, saving his arms except for cuts and bruises. This was significant because it meant the detonators were working, and it was not the mobile trigger that caused his injuries.

In his nightmares, Gill screamed his name, and then everything turned black and he needed to know if it was a memory or a dream.

With the plan of the museum open, he tried to follow his own route. Again, using the witness statements he had been reading.

Before he started, he poured more whisky instead of taking painkillers because it took the edge off his emotional anguish, which was worse than the pain in his leg. Then he sat for a lengthy time, just thinking everything over until the unaccustomed quantity of whisky and exhaustion drove him to bed.

That night was full of vivid, disturbing dreams in

strange locations in which Molly and Geraldine were deep in conversation, always stopping talking when he approached. He woke covered in sweat and troubled by something intangible.

A hot shower, a slice of toast, and his painkillers brought a minor miracle, a logical sequence of events in his mind, although there was more deduction than memory.

Miguel arrived after lunch with a box of groceries. He noticed the papers and put the box in the only available space. Richard looked at him.

"Someone might try again so the supermarket could be dangerous, and Carolina thinks you need to eat."

"We had better solve it soon, then."

His voice had a hint of desperation.

"It's become personal, hasn't it?"

"The professor, Sir Giles and his assistant asked what I remembered of the bombing, and Jane has asked twice. The key has to be in my head, so yes, it's personal."

"So what's all this?"

"I don't know. I came by the case file for the museum and documents from this incident that Chief inspector Landis says I haven't got security clearance for."

"Are you going to tell me how?"

"No."

"John Hollis was on your team in London?"

"Yes, he was."

"Good police officer?"

"Very efficient."

"Talk to me about him. It might be important to understand his motives,"

"He is best described as solid and dependable, and his demeanour and his work record, and his marriage, are all testament to that fact."

"He certainly looks like a copper."

"Yes, and he is one of those rare guys who tied up loose ends, followed deadbeat leads, and kept his paperwork in immaculate order. In addition, his honesty borders on naïve, honest, because it never enters his head to be anything else."

"If it was a wrongful conviction, would he risk putting it right?"

"I don't know. I never saw him take risks, but I remember how much he hated bent coppers."

"Mind if I join you?"

"Should you get involved?"

"The job involves getting information from all kinds of sources and my employers appreciate that. Of course, we get everything we use for prosecution legally, even if the department of justice has to request it. Don't worry, your friend need not fear anything from me because we will go through the correct channels later."

Richard thought for a minute, and his wish to find the truth won over the legal tangle involved. So he nodded and suggested Miguel sit and showed him the time-line and explained his discoveries of the previous evening, summarising and explaining how difficult it was for the bombers to have killed his wife.

"This is the time-line they gave me, but evidence suggests this."

" Someone could have stabbed Gill earlier, but she took an hour to bleed out."

"Yes, it's possible, but unlikely."

Richard handed Miguel the coroner's report.

"Mmm, I see. Weren't you interested at the time?"

"No, I should have been. I was in hospital for a long time when they operated on my leg and I was worried that

I might lose it. But that's not the reason. I couldn't bear the fact that it was my fault that Gill was dead, and I blamed the job and myself."

"So you kept away?"

"I ran away. I bought the cottage while I was still on sick leave and resigned by letter. They awarded a disability pension later. Then I painted, and walked, only a few yards, but effort and the pain stopped me from thinking."

"And now?"

"Today, this has jolted me back to reality and shown me how much I miss the job."

"And the painting?" Miguel pointed to his watercolour rendition of the pilgrim.

"I think that I'm a better painter." Richard didn't know what to say. He was unaccustomed to sharing his private life.

"That is a work of art. I have never seen 'The Way' portrayed so eloquently."

"Can you face your memories yet?"

"I have to. I don't recognise what's happening, but I must remember that night."

Miguel left him to his thoughts then, having pushed him into revealing details which were very personal and, for Richard, still raw.

On Monday morning, the team was back in the office with a palpable sense of frustration. The lack of genuine progress was causing problems, and Miguel had jobs piling up on his desk. The pressure was there to let the British police solve the case.

Richard guessed Jane saw him as a barrier, as he had expressed doubts she was on the right track.

In reality, the review was going to be a handover,

unless something happened soon. He was unsure if something linked these loose ends to the case. The link to the bombing, the location of Molly's body. The attempt on his life and the breaking into of his house were significant, so instead of staying at his desk, he went to his flat to see what else he could remember. His hip and leg were now so stiff and uncomfortable he was glad of the chance to relax. So he propped himself up on his sofa with the reports to read.

Unfortunately, his disturbed sleep caught up with him and he awoke with a start in the late afternoon, having missed the lunchtime briefing. He wanted to know what they discussed. He made himself a coffee and tidied the papers.

In his mind, he was working out who to phone for advice. He was not ready to talk to Miguel again. His telephone Spanish wasn't good enough for Manuel or Chus. Ana and Elvira would both refer him back to the colonel. In the end, he rang Jane for the information, ignoring his sense of dread and trying to be business-like. He told himself that at work, he shouldn't choose with whom he spoke.

"Oh. Hi Richard, how are you?" This friendly, cheerful version of Jane took him by surprise.

"I phoned for an update on the briefing."

"Great. If you're feeling up to it, why not pop round to the office?"

Still puzzled, he agreed.

As he was leaving, his phone pinged a message and two missed calls from Miguel.

"I figured out I had better tell you I shared the details of your attack. Sorry if this causes difficulties, I will explain in the morning."

"Mmm, Wonder why the change of plan?"

Jane was waiting for him when he arrived at the office with coffee and cakes on the conference table. Richard sat without a word, propping his stick on the table, and waited for her to start the conversation, suspecting she had an agenda, and he hoped his silence might force it into the open.

" Look, I am sorry to hear about your accident," she said, her voice full of compassion.

Surprised, he nodded his thanks, but added no more.

"Independence is important, but I am surprised that it hasn't happened before, given your injury. You must consider those who come to your rescue. Isn't it unwise for someone with a disability to be walking on riverside paths late at night?"

The tone was pleasant, suggesting a caring, concerned colleague. Richard took a deep breath but couldn't avoid wincing at the word' disability' because, although he recognised it as the truth, he had never applied it to himself.

"The colonel mentioned I had an accident?"

" Yes, he said that someone had attacked you, but I thought maybe you wouldn't want to admit that your leg was so bad that you fell. After all, you told Sir Giles that didn't you?"

"Yes I did."

"Miguel is using it as an excuse for keeping the enquiry open here in Spain."

"And your suggestion would be?" Richard kept his voice pleasant.

"That it's better to solve it in the UK because there isn't anything to relate it to Spain now. Afterwards I tried to tell him, in private of course, how damaged your leg was and how doctors recommended you to use a wheelchair. But he needs you to be honest regarding your capabilities in person, and you should talk to him.""

She had an ace up her sleeve, he was sure of it.

"In fact, your pension award was based on you being wheelchair bound? Maybe you need a reassessment if you can walk. Would you like me to arrange that for you?"

Richard was silent once again, but this time, shock and anger in combination kept him quiet. Jane passed him his coffee and the plate of cakes.

"Please help yourself as you missed lunch."

Her compassionate tone never faltered, but Richard understood the threat.

"And what else happened at the meeting?" Richard's quiet voice carried none of the emotion he felt.

"Ah yes, two witnesses have come forward. One saw Jack in Portomarín with a woman in a green coat. Someone was present when Jack and Molly argued about the taxi. Another pilgrim has come forward who was in hospital, hence the delay."

"So Jack may have travelled to Portomarín by taxicab."

"Have we found the driver?"

"I haven't heard. They postponed the meeting till the evidence came. I am expecting Miguel to sign everything to me, so that I can go home and...." Jane never got to finish as the sergeant handed her a phone.

"You'll be wanting to take this, from the UK, ma'am."

Richard struggled to his feet and followed John out, allowing her to pick up the call in private.

"It's Molly's friend in Sheffield, Sally something, found dead, sir."

He glanced into the office behind him where the Chief inspector was talking on the phone.

"Was she murdered?"

"Yes."

Jane was rubbing her neck and pacing and her confident air of controlling everything was gone. He didn't ask what else they had said. He thanked the sergeant and left. This big review meeting would not happen tomorrow, he was sure of that. He set off in search of Miguel to tell him the news.

# CHAPTER TWENTY

## *John Hollis*

When Jane chose sergeant Hollis to go with her as a bagman, it surprised him as much as it surprised his colleagues. He transferred to her unit the year before in the wake of the museum bombing, and he didn't always fit in, because he was an old-fashioned, honest policeman. Chief Inspector Landis had a reputation of being a player. They gave some cases priority, because the squad understood some people were more important. John was uncomfortable around her, although he tried hard not to show it, acknowledging her brilliant mind and her career path, which was more of a blazing trail than a steady climb.

The team cut corners, unnerving him, not because he was naïve, but because he believed the British bobby should continue as the gold standard for the world. When he first transferred, he hoped to find proof she had falsified evidence in the museum bombing case. What he discovered was that she was cleverer than he imagined.

Just before he left for Spain, he discovered that Chief Inspector Harris was there assisting the local detectives and saw an opportunity.

John and his colleagues were disappointed when Richard vanished before the trial, having heard stories he was ill and could no longer cope, and that he'd lost his memory. That's why he didn't give evidence. The sergeant had worked for Richard and trusted him. His former boss was eccentric and quiet, but they could trust him to fix things.

He had gone home and told his wife that he was putting his career on the line and if his old supervisor was too ill or refused to get involved, they might lose everything. Then he took a deep breath and shared his plan with a like-minded colleague.

Now he was here. It was more difficult than he expected. He had done as much as he dared and John needed to make sure his former chief Inspector was on board before the handover.


On Tuesday morning, Miguel attempted once again to narrow the case to a terrorist threat. He asked for information on the IRA, from worldwide colleagues he often conferred with. They worked together often, defying the politics involved, and were getting results. A word in the right ear, a nod toward the truth and shared data all helped when your criminals performed without national borders.

"I just heard from a friend in the intelligence community. The IRA doesn't exist. The leads Jane Landis gave us points to a business association in Russia and Iran, calling themselves RIBA, who are working together for cooperation between the countries regarding the sale of oil. They aim to make a more ethical market and lessen the

Saudi influence. They aren't warmongers or radicals as far as anyone knows and membership crosses religious boundaries. Every time we get additional information, I have said to look deeper and nothing emerges. We must accept there is nothing and they are not terrorists."

The colonel was pacing the room, and Richard sensed his friend's frustration.

"Have you told Jane this?"

"No."

"What about the professor's statement and Jane's belief in it?"

"Either diversion or mistake, we need to know which."

"How certain are you? How safe are your sources?"

"Ninety-five per cent sure and my sources are excellent. We are being played."

"What if I dig in the UK? I can start in Sheffield with Sally James's death. Maybe we missed something because I'm not convinced by co-incidence," said Richard.

It's dangerous and time is short and I am under pressure to sign this off to the British police."

"I hope you don't want to, because my opinion of chief Inspector Landis has not changed."

"No, the information.... some piece of evidence is nagging at my mind... It's the link with you that's bothering me. But if it comes down to Muslim terrorists from Britain, Jane should take the case home."

"But what?" He watched the expression change on Miguel's face.

"I think she is leading us in the wrong direction."

"How long can you hold off for?"

"48 hours at most."

Despite the risk involved, Richard found himself on a plane to England with John on Wednesday morning. It was their task to get the details of Sally James's murder, keep the rest of the team informed, and take another statement from Tom Miller. It was to be a flying visit.

Jane argued it was a UK matter and she could go to Sheffield on her way to London. They delayed the final review until they were better informed. Miguel agreed to sign off on local involvement if Sally's death did not add other intelligence, which suggested Spanish involvement.

Richard was uncertain how to talk to John about the bombing.

"Any idea what was in the file that Chief Inspector Landis gave to the CPS in the London museum explosive case?" he asked on the plane.

"That's what I hoped that you'd ask, sir! What do you want to know?" A mixture of excitement and relief was unequivocal in John's expression.

How did the prosecution get a conviction? The evidence I've seen appears to clear the men in jail?"

"There have been others wondering that." John replied without further comment. Richard waited for the sergeant to say more, but he remained silent.

There was little conversation afterwards, each lost in their own thoughts, until he understood why John's actions made sense.

"Were you hoping to jog my memory so I would have a clear picture of events as I experienced them? Then I could give a witness statement, enough to get the case reopened."

"Oh, that kind of decision is above my pay grade, but no one likes a stitch up. You, sir, if I remember, used to be very emphatic about that." John emphasised the sir, giving him the impression that he had protested about the way the event was handled and a senior officer had reprimanded him, and he wasn't alone in that.

There was silence again, Richard going over and over events in his mind, wondering why they killed Molly outside his house and was it a warning to keep quiet? He considered why people were asking what he remembered. At least, he understood now why it was important. Public speculation would force an enquiry.

When they landed at Heathrow, the pair dashed to get the Sheffield train so it didn't arise again. John gave his seat to a woman with a crying baby. The rest of the journey he spent gazing through the steamed-up window as the dull grey landscape disappeared into the evening dusk. He had grown unused to crowded trains and used to fresh mountain air and realised the extent that he thought of Galicia as home.

They took a taxi to their hotel, one of the many bland but clean budget establishments that are everywhere these days. The place smelt of cleaning fluid, and the paintwork and the lights were bright. They had a lot to do when they arrived. They introduced themselves to Detective Inspector Riley, whose Yorkshire accent took some getting used to. She was direct and looked Richard in the eye when she gave them a summary of the findings.

Sally had worked past her normal time and agreed to meet friends in a pub in town. She never made it and we found her body that night beside a car park. Someone had stabbed her and taken her phone and bag so that it appeared to be a mugging.

"There is some security camera footage from outside the parking area. A couple approached sally. Then look closely as she appears to recognise them and it looks as though they offered her a lift."

Despite no clear picture of the woman, Sally's boyfriend recognised them as a couple they met on the Camino. A different camera, an hour later, showed two men leaving the area.

"Tom Miller told us about your investigation. So we contacted you in case of a connection to the murder of Molly Hambleton. DCI Jane Landis was sure it was a coincidence, but I see you think it has significance."

"Could we talk to the boyfriend?" asked Richard.

"Of course, I'll set it up for first thing in the morning," said Inspector Riley.

"A pub or an Indian Restaurant?"

"Oh, both please!"

Richard cheered up at the thought, remembering the things that he missed. Pubs and ethnic food being at the top of his list, so they walked into a busier part of town, recognising they needed a taxi back. Sheffield came as a pleasant surprise, a bustling modern city full of students and locals alike. Before long, they found a friendly pub, a traditional converted coach house unlike modern trendy establishments with vast open spaces with a warehouse style, designer beers, gins, and cocktails. The White Rose comprised a string of tiny rooms all linked together, so they settled by a fire and, as the establishment served food, they stayed for the evening.

Neither were conversationalists, content just to sit and think or stare into their beer. John relaxed. He had got his message across and his responsibility had ended there. It unnerved Richard, but bigger issues were at stake. Issues that resembled a lamp glimpsed through the fog, a hazy shape in a vague direction.

What he couldn't remember bothered him, and the more the pressure, the harder it became to focus.

But here, the weariness and the warm comfortable atmosphere caused his mind to wander as he remembered the good times with Gill and friends and the familiar atmosphere, so peculiar to Britain, was surprisingly comforting.

They interviewed Tom on Thursday morning and he was shocked, but calm and determined to help. He recognised three of the four people in the videos.

"The name sounded posh, double barrelled. I wish I remembered more. He lived in my hall but knocked around campus with some rum looking skinheads."

"But he wasn't a skinhead, or was he?"

"No, always looked smart. That's why I remember the contrast in styles. A friend told me he had been to Eton, but I'm not sure."

Inspector Riley promised to tell them when she received more information. And afterwards, they left for London.


An hour later, when they were sitting on the train, Richard noticed John couldn't hide the satisfaction he felt at going home. The sergeant had married late and found the happiness that few ever achieved. They arranged to meet the following day.

"The older I get, the harder I find it to leave. Where will you go?"

Richard suspected John felt guilty because he hadn't asked his former boss to stay with him. It was unusual for a sergeant to offer a chief inspector hospitality unless the friendship was old and well established, but he knew Susan, the sergeant's wife, would ask where he was staying. After she sent a card when Gill died with a touching message, he had been to thank her. She had bustled around the kitchen getting tea and cake and made him welcome, with no awkwardness because he was

John's superior or grieving.

Richard sensed his discomfort. "I'm visiting with an old acquaintance. Well, she was a close friend of Gill's and I've rather neglected friendships."

"OK, we'll share a cab," said John with obvious relief.

The night before, he had contacted Patricia Birch, his wife's closest friend and a psychologist, a specialist in trauma, hoping she might help with his memory. The call had delighted her, and she invited him to stay, so he made the arrangements.

"No need for a taxi. I'm going in the opposite direction. One tube stop, then I can walk."

"With respect, sir, I will never forgive myself if something happened..."

Richard blanched. He had forgotten about the danger because everything was normal and familiar. He was thinking of Patricia, who had been to medical school with Gill. A clinical psychologist who married a doctor twenty years her senior who she met at her first hospital job. The marriage made them both happy, and they had a son at university. They were at Gill's funeral. A year later, when he read of Stephen's death, he sent condolences, but couldn't face going to the burial.

The reason he contacted Patricia now was because he wanted something, which caused him to feel guilty.

"There are lodgers," she teased, "so don't go thinking it would be inappropriate." The couple were colourful liberals, and his old-fashioned, deep faith came with an overblown conscience.

His emotions were mixed even as they got into the black cab because, as a professional trauma counsellor, she knew how he could access his memory and he wanted to pick her brains. He was afraid that staying there would remind him of Gill and their life in London, and he had run away from that memory.

The taxi stopped outside Patricia's house, but on the opposite side of the narrow road that circled the large central gardens in a once elegant and exclusive city square. Most of the houses in the square are apartments. The multi-million pound cost of a flat here ensured it was smart, but gone were the servants, gardeners, carriages and parasols, leaving a suggestion that they had left better days behind. Patricia's house was one of the few remaining with a single front door.

Now three absent Russian millionaires and Patricia lived in undivided houses, the rest were apartments. He was thinking of these things when he paid the taxi driver and said goodbye to John, and didn't pay enough attention to his immediate surroundings. He picked up his bag awkwardly because of his stick. Then, unbalanced by the weight, he stumbled backwards on a manhole cover, steadying himself on the back of the cab. At that moment, a black hatchback shot past, hitting Richard, knocking him and clipping the taxi's wing mirror.

# CHAPTER TWENTY-ONE

*Another accident?*

Richard opened his eyes without being aware that he had first closed them. The taxi driver, John and Patricia, were looking at him with worried expressions and he laughed for no sensible reason, an escapee from Alice's Adventures in Wonderland. The laughter did not meet with his concerned friends' approval and he could hear murmurs of concern.

"He's in shock" and "The ambulance is coming." He attempted to rise, but with no stick and with people so close, his attempt was comical. A grown man squirming on a filthy London street underneath a classic black cab watched by friends struck him as funny anew, so reminiscent of Charlie Chaplin or Mr Bean. He was laughing now, and only the actual arrival of the paramedics focused his mind. He protested, asking for help to stand. The paramedic refused to allow him to move without a neck brace and kept him quiet until he was in the ambulance. The hatchback drove past again, but everyone ignored both his comments about that and protests about the hospital. He and Patricia found themselves with a long wait in A&E. The duty doctor suggested that he stayed the night, but when he refused, he looked relieved and Richard signed a 'left against doctor's advice form' using the bed shortage as an excuse.

Later, back at Patricia's.

"Next time, could you be less dramatic about your arrival?"

Patricia grinned, swirling the wine in her glass.

Richard blushed and apologised again.

"I am so sorry, and to make it worse, I'm here to request a favour."

"Feeding you take-away in front of the fire would have horrified Stephen. He would tell me to give you anything you asked for. At least the drink is decent, so let's enjoy our dinner, then you ask everything."

Richard had a bath and changed while Patricia phoned for takeout food and opened a bottle, and though he ached from his bruises, the flames were warm against his face. He was comfortable and his muscles, which had been tense for weeks, relaxed.

"Could I tell you the entire story? I'll be as brief as possible."

She was a good listener, only interrupting to clarify a point.

"Why didn't you come before?"

"I thought of it, but then Stephen..."

" So, you were too raw yourself to face someone else's grief."

He nodded, dropping his eyes away.

"Stephen was ill for a long while. I was glad of the time we had, but I spent much of my grief caring for him. Death when it came was a relief. For both of us. I miss him, though."

Richard just nodded.

"It's not the same because you lost Gill without warning, and you blame yourself. But regrets don't change anything, and mourning isn't about blame. The memories and love will remain. Yes, Stephen and I had the blessing of saying goodbye, but watching him fade away...." She shuddered. "Being so alone afterwards, we both have that in common."

"Is that the reason for the lodgers? It's not... that you need them."

"Oh, how English you are. No, I'm wealthy enough. Stephen's family is.. well, you know, together with us having highly paid jobs and only one son. When Stephen was alive, we were always too busy working to spend much. No paying guests keep the house alive and pay for maintenance, there is a lot. There is a housekeeper and a starving medical student who looks after me and who you'll meet tomorrow."

There was a silence for a moment.

"If you want to recover your memory, there are techniques that can be used. Shall we talk tomorrow?"

"Yes please, I am no longer going anywhere. I think my life might depend on it."

The doctor told him to visit out-patients and not fly until they cleared him, due to the danger of an aneurysm. Patricia made him welcome and organised plans to cancel her clients for a few days to spend time with him.

On Friday, just before lunch, John arrived at Patricia's to see him.

"The lads found a black hatchback on waste ground, burnt out, stolen by joyriders and not connected to the incident in Spain. The sergeant brought news and photocopies of the evidence lists from the bombing. They learnt Jane Landis, along with the professor, was returning to London. The case is not active now unless something else happens.

Miguel's team was going to move on. Though on alert for developments.

Richard was defeated, not least because he was not safe. He had no doubt that the accident wasn't a joyrider, but a deliberate attempt to kill him. Sheffield informed him the press had photos, and a reconstruction was being considered. That, thank goodness, was still an active case. Jane, however, said the link to Molly was tenuous and, apart from asking to be informed of changes, was taking no further interest. Everywhere he turned, he hit a brick wall.

He could not get hold of Miguel, who was busy sorting his team out.

So, he paced, or limped, around Patricia's elegant drawing room, then borrowed her key to the central square and paced there, where there was space and air. After living in Galicia, he could never describe London's air as fresh, but it was better than nothing, and the garden soothed him. In there were signs of hope. The trees wore a halo of green, not yet clothed, but no longer naked. Daffodils adorned the grassy banks, still tight and erect, with only a glimpse of their yellow bonnets but promising a glorious display. In fact, in every corner of this square spring was evident, in the colours delicate pinks, yellows and whites, but poised for summer colours.

No investigation in his past had depended on him. None had been personal, none had pierced him. He never felt threatened despite being threatened. Much was familiar and much was different, but his life had evolved, and he needed to decide what was next. The story had changed before, when he married, when he joined the police force. When he and Gill discovered they couldn't have children, when she died and when he moved to Galicia.

The first step was to sort this case out and untangle himself from it so, he sat and thought through that day in the London Museum and this time instead of a blank space he found himself with a jumble of images, of people, a rucksack, no two, wires, parcels, push button mobiles, conversations, Gill screaming, him running, immense pain, then nothing as his shoulders relaxed as the weight he carried went. He had an idea that the memories needed to be tested because the picture was incomplete. Patricia was back when he returned and they ate lunch downstairs in the kitchen. The lodgers were working and Mrs B., the housekeeper, had left sandwiches, declaring she was too busy to eat with them.

"I've remembered some things, but not everything."

"It's amazing how often facing a situation releases memories. Do you wish to talk?" Patricia asked.

"I'd like to talk about Gill, too, and I haven't been able to. After that, I need to research."

"Can I help with the research?"

"Would you want to?"

"Yes, yes I would."

Both Patricia and her house were elegant. Her consulting office was in the old drawing-room, painted pale yellow with ornate coving. Huge floor-to-ceiling windows allowed light to pour in and although a gas insert had replaced the coals, the fireplace was original. Two comfortable sofas were on either side of a coffee table. Beside the fire place, was a unit with a sink and drink making facilities. More books and an antique desk sat between the windows with a cupboard, in which Richard found a modern filing arrangement with a complicated-looking lock.

"I need clients to feel at home and comfortable here. Because in Britain, people are afraid of psychologists. They view mental illness or trauma is a weakness and they are ashamed, and so I try to put individuals at ease.

Let's make a cup of coffee and then we'll talk."

"Didn't you work in the hospital?"

" Yes, I did, but when Stephen was ill, I cut my hospital hours and took private clients to be at home. When he died, I converted the house, more to keep busy than anything. The coach building and stables already had tenants. The four upstairs bedrooms were given a shower room, and I cleared out the servants' quarters in the attic and created two small flats and a guest suite.

Gwen, (Mrs B), lives there and Joanna, who you haven't met and who is a medical student and helps around the home. I redecorated this floor, the guest suite we had done for Stephen. Stephen had a small bathroom in his bedroom and it demanded little work. If you remember, we used this as the formal dining room and it's still new to me, but the changes help avoid painful memories. The latest tenant moved in last week, but I love folk filling the house."

Richard understood that she needed to keep busy and have a purpose.

He himself was an introvert, never needing others.

That was until Gill had died, and then he understood. Everyone needs human contact, isolation can destroy your self confidence, and that loneliness is agonising.

He remembered the last time he had been here. Sitting at the table drinking wine from Stephen's excellent cellar. He, as usual, was uncomfortable in the presence of the family's wealth. It had never affected Gill, though. She and Patricia were like schoolgirls when they were together, sharing stories, and laughing at everything and everyone. Stephen was a gracious host, an extrovert, a mimic, and a teller of tales that got taller as the evening progressed. The women were opposites: Patricia tall and elegant, Gill practical, down to earth, and untidy looking.

Richard smiled at a memory.

"You are the only person who calls me beautiful," Gill said often.

She had her patients and as an intensive care paediatrician, she cared too much for them. She was never still, loved being outdoors, disliked shopping and never wore make-up. Patricia, tall, quiet and a listener by nature, was different.

They talked all afternoon, not logically. But of Gill and how guilty he was, how often they both missed her. The museum and the medal he had won, and he admitted he felt a fraud. They spoke of his leg, his fears for the future, art, and his home in Galicia and last, about the bombing and this time he remembered, and remembering hurt so much.

He phoned the colonel, suggesting he come over, not with Jane and the professor. Maybe the following day, Sunday. That gives us a chance to talk before the working week starts.

Richard could only ask that Miguel trust him.

He and Patricia then researched into the night. The next morning they left for the Westminster exhibition, staying for two hours, just watching and listening. Because they were so interested, the enthusiastic young guide invited them to look at a special screening of a video. A video about Britain's potential outlook, not open to the public.

After watching, they knew for sure. It gave them a vision of the future that was beautifully edited and filmed and at first sounded innocuous. Everyone was white, people with disabilities chose sterilisation or euthanasia, workers were deferential and happy with their lot, and so it went. Always summer, cheerful music, harmony.

"I didn't appreciate that mindset still existed."

"I wish you didn't have to know now. It could be worse than I ever expected."

When they got back to London, Richard prepared a statement and posted it to John at his home, a precaution against another accident. They recorded his memories and his conclusions. But for court, he needed proof, and that was the next step and Monday morning's job.

# CHAPTER TWENTY-TWO

## *Miguel's frustration.*

*In the meantime, in Spain.*

The day Richard and Sergeant Hollis left was endless for Miguel. Jane Landis had grown in confidence and victory for her was taking the case to London. She was treating him, and not the murderer, as her opponent and her confident winding up of things added to his sense of despair. He sat in his small office and leaned back in his chair. There were piles of paper everywhere on every surface.

The whole thing frustrated him and if he was being honest with himself, he had experienced nothing but frustration since this case started. He had wanted to spend time with his family while working from home. By home, he meant this office and now he was more conflicted after this experiment. At the moment, he had neither a career nor a home life. Chus and Manuel must be keen to return to the city because they asked when they were leaving.

Never had he handed an unsolved case to a local force: it meant failure. Sure, he had left them to tidy up the loose ends. Not this, though. Total defeat on his home patch was painful, and the only thing remaining was to write a report detailing his investigation. He had better start by sorting out this wretched paperwork.

When he looked at his watch, he decided that tomorrow was soon enough. A relaxed dinner and a glass of wine with Carolina were bound to cheer him up. Then, he would tell her that their brief experiment of country living had failed, thus leaving her to select whether to accept a long distance husband or move back to Madrid. That wasn't fair to her. He needed to resolve what career he wanted and what to sacrifice to pursue it.

He left for work early the next morning, but not with enthusiasm. Paperwork was his least favourite task, and there was a significant amount to do. Computerisation was wonderful, but at this stage, juggling emails, on-line forms, and paper reports was a thing he hated. There was something satisfying having piles of files and watching them disappear as you worked through them, and frustrating in knowing that you've seen what you needed but not remembered the format.

He sighed and collected the paperwork in his office and his laptop, and took it to the conference room. It only took two journeys because Chus and Manuel helped. They piled everything onto the central table and Miguel turned to thank them, knowing that they had their work to do before they could return to the city.

Chus spoke first: "It's a blow, handing this over, boss. We were wondering if we helped with sorting and doing the final reports we could find our mistakes?"

That surprised him. "I thought you were itching to get back to Madrid."

A look passed between them he couldn't fathom, but Manuel just said,

"Feels like failure at the moment, sir, and we'd rather know why."

Once again, Miguel's team encouraged him.

"OK then, let's start with the crime scene and initial witnesses. Chus, you take the medical report, Manuel the witness statements, and I'll look at the forensics."

Manuel said. "I'll write notes for the record just to ensure someone can read them and we'll get Ana to type it up. And then your handwriting or your computer skills won't slow us down."

He was looking at Miguel.

"No, we can't ask her to do that. She has worked her socks off as admin and interpreter as it is."

"Somebody can," said Chus, grinning at Manuel. "But you will need to clear it with her duty-sergeant, boss."

Again, it startled him, realising he had missed something here.

Ana's shift didn't start until four thirty, but it was OK with her supervisor and Ana arrived half an hour later, looking pleased but not surprised. Not the normal expression of someone about to do unpaid overtime, he noted.

Once they started work, it was less tedious than he imagined. They sorted out the piles of paper and linked them to relevant computer files.

He was the first to discover something.

"There are green fibres from the fence: Technical outdoors, similar to Gortex. Molly's jacket was red and Richard's navy blue. Do the witness statements mention the colour of people's clothing?"

\* \* \*

"Yes. Give me a minute to locate them," said Manuel, sorting through notes on his desk.

"Ah, here. A woman in green reported by that private investigator and later was seen with Jack Clarke in Portomarín. No ID, no follow-up because we were pursuing the political angle by the second sighting.

"OK. Let's start a list. Can we get the white-board and pens back?"

Ana rushed off to find them. Miguel had forgotten they were here to wrap things up and write last reports, and his team members looked and smiled at him encouragingly as he suspected that neither gained a very high opinion of Chief Inspector Jane Landis, whose responsibility it was now.

Manuel was next: "A witness who saw the argument between Jack and Molly, but no statement."

Then Chus: "We have the medical report evidence that the killer stabbed Molly when they were facing each other. There was a bruise where the knife hilt pierced her sternum, and no holes in her jacket. The blade may have been a sharpened paper cutter, and it looks as though she knew her attacker, or at least been comfortable enough to stand and chat with them. The statement also suggested that she may not have been wearing her rucksack."

Miguel's head was in his hands.

"What have we been doing? These are basic, very basic errors. How did we miss them?"

"Chasing political ghosts, boss."

"OK, there are less than forty-eight hours before I hand this case over. Richard gets back the day after tomorrow and Jane leaves the same time. I'll try to extend the period, but with only the four of us, I don't know how useful it will be."

He looked up. He didn't need to ask if they agreed.

"Shouldn't we tell Chief Inspector Landis what we are doing?" asked Chus, twiddling her hair, conflicted because she didn't like the woman, but believed that female officers should stick together when possible.

"No," said Manuel and Miguel in unison. "And if she asks, we are preparing the last report, which we will email to her."

Chus was tapping the table now, picking things up and putting them down again.

"We've missed evidence by not following our routine working pattern. Because I've allowed Chief Inspector Landis to lead meetings, in the belief that we could work as a single team. I believe she has distracted us. I'm not sure if it was deliberate, my mistake has cost too much. We should have worked as normal and held separate briefings to include her and even the professor. Where is he, by the way?"

"Are they together as in... together...?"

" What?" asked Miguel, no fan of gossip.

"If it explains the professor's intrusion, it will be useful."

"It's only that, Ana and I...," said Manuel.

Chus sniggered.

Manuel blushed and continued. "They were sharing a table in the Italian and it was very cosy."

"That's funny, I saw him having dinner with that PA, Sir Giles's assistant, Geraldine. I thought they might be an item."

"Maybe he just likes the company of women."

"Let's see what else we missed."

The following couple of hours, they looked through everything. Ana helping Manuel with the witness statements. By lunchtime, there were several leads to follow. Do they produce a new list or clear the leads first? Could they find a new direction?.

So, he typed the salient points and emailed everyone. After a moment's hesitation, to Richard and he realised he was hiding evidence from Jane. Wrong, and yet instinct was telling him that mentioning it to her was a mistake.

As though his thoughts summoned her, she appeared in the doorway, clipboard in hand, hesitating when she saw the four of them, looking surprised.

"What's happening?" she asked.

"Just organising the information for the handover and adding our last reports," said Miguel.

"Oh yes, of course. Have you heard from Richard? I was expecting Sergeant Hollis to phone, but he hasn't yet."

"Nothing concrete. Sheffield caught a man on camera near the place where they killed Sally. Tom thinks he recognises him as someone they met over here and shared a couple of meals with. But until we have identified him and linked him to the scene, it could be irrelevant. Richard will contact me when they learn more. It explains the lack of contact from John."

"So it's just a mugging gone wrong." Jane was brisk. "Let me know if you hear otherwise," and she turned and marched along the corridor.

The four of them stood and watched her retreating.

Chus spoke first. "Does she believe it, or does she want us to believe it?"

"Let's break. Anyone who wants to join me for lunch, could you wait here till I get my coat?" said Miguel, and they were glad of the chance to have lunch and chat without pressure for an hour.

Half way through the afternoon, they had a phone call from sergeant Hollis telling them of Richard's accident. He had phoned the chief inspector and told her they were waiting for follow up information from Sheffield and a car had hit Richard. When Jane left to tell the team, she was gloating.

"When will that man realise that his accident disabled him? It would be better if he returned to painting pictures."

John had phoned the colonel, anticipating his agreement that it was another attack. He was not disappointed.

"We were taking a risk. Next time, he won't be so lucky. I'm not sure why he's alive, because these people mean business."

Miguel tried to ring Richard, but he had turned his phone off so he emailed instead, outlining their plans and hoping everything was well.

All of them worked late into the night, pursuing leads. Selecting two each to chase up, whoever finished first taking an extra one. They got information, but ended with nothing new, expecting the following day to be a repeat, except with less enthusiasm.

Jane decided not to wait for their reports and returned to London early with the professor. Her going gave an air of finality.

John phoned and reassured them that Richard, although shaken, was fine, but needed to stick around for permission to fly.

They made a new list after returning to the information. With Jane gone, they wrote on the white board without fear, follow-up items from yesterday, and today's finds. By lunchtime, they had organised everything, and were following up points they had missed. The room was busy and quiet.

Miguel looked at what they had left and at his team. "Lets choose three leads. Manuel and Ana take one, Chus another, and me the last. We've got five hours to come up with something."

"I'll pick up the waterlogged documents. This sketch looks like a mind-map and it might give us some links."

"We will do more research on the professor, starting with his links to Sheffield since we know they arrested him there..."

"OK, I'll finish the follow-up on the woman in green."

They were hoping for a miracle.

# CHAPTER TWENTY-THREE

## *Seeing things more clearly*

The bar owner, who had seen the woman in green, described her to a sketch artist. Miguel assumed Richard could get him a second drawing from Dave Bromley, the private investigator. He hoped, as an artist, he was able to draw from a description, but wasn't certain.

Manuel was still trawling through records for more information on the professor.

The mind map diagram was water damaged, but Chus had resurrected part of it. Unfortunately, the headings were unreadable. The colonel, however, was sure it meant something significant.

He was sitting staring at a copy when his colleague phoned.

"Richard, *hombre,* how are you?"

"I'm fine, really. And I have news."

The latest attack on his friend worried Miguel. He was sure it was an attack and wasn't comfortable handing over the event unless they stopped.

Richard explained he had remembered the night of the bombing.

He sounded excited, telling Miguel once he and Patricia had put everything in order and had a coherent story he would tell him. He wanted the colonel to stick with the case.

"Buy us a little time because we are close to finding some solid information."

He agreed, but pointed out that the evidence available was tenuous and they needed something solid to follow up.

"What about the woman in green? You told me in your email that someone described her."

"Ahh, yes, and you could help me. A barman gave me a sketch. Will you visit the private investigator that Sir Giles used and get a picture, or better, another drawing?"

"Of course, that's one reason I rang. His card is in my wallet, but I can give you a general picture now. Dave Bromley mistook Geraldine for the woman in green. It startled him, so there must be a strong likeness."

"Wasn't it Geraldine who hired him?"

"Yes, it was. But he had never seen her. They spoke over the phone."

"They arrived the Friday after the murder, didn't they?"

"Well, Sir Giles did. Might Geraldine be the woman in green?"

"No, I guess it would be impossible but I am at the stage of clutching at straws now," he sighed, then asked: "What do you mean Sir Giles did? Didn't they travel together?"

"No, she arrived the day before to prepare for her boss."

"In these days of the internet? Perhaps she is worth

looking into. If you can, get a sketch anyway."

"On another note, Tom Miller recognised both people in the CCTV footage taken near the site of Sally's murder. But still only unconfirmed names," said Richard.

"That's interesting. It was the Sheffield police who arrested the professor for his fascist activities. That was years ago, but we aren't aware of any current ties. Manuel and Ana are checking now."

"Another coincidence. I wonder where he did his academic work and whether he had links with the university. Patricia and I saw his exhibition, and it is relevant to the case."

They rang off, but Miguel found that his enthusiasm and the urgency had returned.

"Manuel, can you check passenger lists from the UK for Geraldine, his assistant?" and then speaking more to himself.

"It would make more sense of this diagram if it involved her," he shook himself. Trying to manipulate facts to fit random pieces of potential evidence was an enthusiastic rookie mistake, so he would let this play out.

"Can we watch interviews with Sally and Tom again? I feel one of them gave us a name." said Miguel to no person in particular.

Geraldine wasn't recorded on any flight into Galicia on Wednesday, Thursday or Friday of that week. Manuel even checked flights into Madrid for those days in case she had flown to the capital and then taken the train. Her involvement looked likely, as she must have been in Spain for a week or more.

More digging found the professor did both his undergraduate and Ph.D. work in Sheffield. The university had distanced itself from him after his arrest. News reports suggested he had stepped down from an honorary position because of his involvement in, or leadership of, a vicious underground fascist organisation. They suspected them of several racist attacks, other than the one at which they had arrested Lord Bonham. It was part of a series of events in cities. They had no evidence the unit had disbanded, or the duke had disassociated himself. The group has gone underground with no arrests, although recently the speaker at a rally was traced to them, but working within the law. These days, they prefer to stir up racial hatred until they created an explosive atmosphere, and leaving others to do the damage.

"So, is there a link between Geraldine and the professor?"

"No," said Chus, "Other than the Westminster exhibition, and on the surface it looks legitimate, but I'll keep on it."

"This means I can buy some time, guys. You are due in Madrid tomorrow, and me at the weekend. I'll spend my leave on this, if you want to go, but an extra two days might crack it open and I won't get us more than that, anyway."

Manuel and Chus exchanged a glance and shuffled their feet, each waiting for the other to speak, neither meeting the colonel's eye.

"OK, I accept it. You're keen to return because it's a frustrating case, and Sarria is from the last century." He put up his hands. "You are right, of course. We should hand it over and return to normal."

"We were wondering if we might base the unit here?" Manuel caught the expression on Miguel's face. "No, I guess it is a stupid scheme."

"Are you serious? You think this too, Chus?" asked Miguel.

"Other than Juan, the entire team thinks it's a good idea. Carmen was talking of leaving after the baby because she wants her children to enjoy a more rural lifestyle and a move here means she can do both. José would be glad of a cheaper place to live so that he could buy more electrical equipment. Juan is a city boy, but even he says he will purchase a flat in Lugo and commute between here and Madrid, on the high-speed train."

Miguel looked so shocked that Manuel and Chus stumbled over their rehearsed speech.

"It's not our decision or yours, but we cover this area...," said Manuel

"Of course, we would need to solve this case...," added Chus.

"But if you are against the idea...."

"But we hoped since your family was here...."

They halted, still unable to read Miguel's face.

"I thought you would prefer Madrid." They were smiling now. "Leave it with me then. No promises, though."

There was a sigh of relief and the day looked brighter altogether, the morning's plodding lethargy gone.

Miguel phoned his boss and explained the position.

"How do the British police feel about this?" asked the general.

"I haven't inquired."

"Why? You've got a chief inspector sharing a bloody office with you. You are better than this."

"Jane Landis has flown home. We overlooked something and when we were writing reports, we came up with some fresh evidence."

"So now you're asking for time to cover up sloppy work?"

"Yes. For the case, our reputation, and a desire that this doesn't come back to bite us." Miguel was in danger of damaging his mobile. He was gripping it so hard.

"Twenty-four hours and get on the phone to London. Bugger up the politics with Brexit happening and all our heads will roll."

The line went dead before the colonel finished.

"Didn't go well then, boss? Don't worry because we are due some holiday if the worst happens."

Miguel relaxed at Chus' cheerful tone. "That's another day, anyway. Now, where were we?"

"Someone from Sheffield CID is getting back to me," said Manuel.

"I'm waiting to hear from one of Sir Giles's parliamentary researchers, who acts as his PA when Geraldine is on leave."

"Gosh, you haven't alerted Geraldine, have you? When we question her, we don't want rehearsed answers."

"No, both are in Northern Ireland."

"Ask Sheffield if they have names for the CCTV pictures yet," said Miguel.

"You'll need to interpret, or take, the call. Ana's interpreting for Chus," replied Manuel.

"I'll interpret. Sometimes we get more information from a less formal call. Where are we on the professor?"

"That's proving difficult because his family is influential, and he has been careful to keep himself out of the public eye. As he works for himself and is wealthy enough to self-finance his projects, he is free to come and go as he pleases. He employs his brother to run the household and estate, so he is not needed there."

"Can we track him through his exhibition?" asked Miguel.

"Again, he employs a manager to oversee everything, so no one records his movements. I'm getting a list of his speaking engagements, but we need someone on the ground if we want more information."

Chus's phone rang. It was the parliamentary researcher. And she was chatty. Molly and Geraldine were very close, and she had helped Molly plan the Camino trip and buy the walking gear as she was on leave.

"I booked flights and hotel rooms for Sir Giles because up to the Northern Ireland trip, Geraldine was off work.

"Do you know Lord Bonham?"

"Yes, I do. He's a friend of Sir Giles and visits their home. As I'm based in the parliamentary office, I don't see him often. Between you and me, I think Geraldine has a bit of a crush on him because she always rushes to take his calls and meets him if he comes to Westminster. Of course, he was Molly's godfather and I expect her death devastated him. Geraldine was furious that he didn't make it back to the funeral. It's the only time I've heard her disagree with him."

"Well, there is our link. What does he know about Molly's murder?"

"If she was his god-daughter, he couldn't involve himself with her killing, could he?" said Chus, who was from a very large, very close family and could never understand that kind of violence within families, however often it happened.

Miguel looked across and grinned.

"You know how that works in practice," he said.

A lot of violent crime occurred inside the families they investigated, and this was an oft repeated exchange.

A detective in the Sheffield anti-terrorism squad phoned. The conversation was brief. There was no trouble with the Duke since the original incident. The files are here because we suspect a connection with the Sally James murder. We recognised some of the names. And they had identified Molly Hambleton as a member from old intelligence records. Chief Inspector Jane Landis was in charge of the case, and he was going to phone her.

"Did the group involve Sally James and Tom Miller?"

"No, I checked and there is nothing recorded, although they haven't caused trouble recently, so we haven't taken a close interest."

"Do you think that Tom Miller is part of that organisation now?"

"Speak to Inspector Riley, in charge of the murder enquiry."

The phone rang again before he could process that information.

"Miguel, you should come over here. I have disturbing news," said Richard.

"About the bombing or about Molly Hambleton?"

"Both, and there is a close link. Better to talk in person. Can you trust me on this? I now know what happened, and it makes no sense. There was only one individual who could have killed Gill. I don't know why, maybe the same character killed Molly.

"The team has not been idle and we may have made similar discoveries. I'll book a flight, but why talk to me and not the Chief Inspector?"

"Because she is close to Lord Bonham, and we can't trust either of them."

Miguel caught the reluctance. "OK, I'll see you tomorrow."

Miguel's phone had been on speaker.

"Do you think it involves Jane Landis?"

"Who never wanted us involved," said Chus.

"Why did the professor come?" asked Manuel.

"Can you remain here? the situation is odd and I'm worried about where it is heading."

# CHAPTER TWENTY-FOUR

*Miguel sorts things out.*

The weather in Santiago was grey and wet on Sunday when Miguel caught his flight, echoing his mood. The crowded plane held a mixture of returning pilgrims, British ex-pats and Spanish workers who had jobs in London. Today, clouds blocked the sun and the ground for the entire trip. There was nothing visible from the windows, and turbulence meant he couldn't unfasten his seatbelt. That and his bulk imprisoned him, so his muscles were stiff and sore by the time he stepped onto the wet tarmac at Stansted Airport. Sleet was replacing the drizzle as he strode across the tarmac to the arrivals building.

The drive round the M25 was a bleak prospect. The journey was so last minute; he discovered that the car they had allocated him was a large seven/seater designed for families on a budget, with cheap looking plastic knobs and inadequate heating.

As he expected, he had two hours of end-to-end cars, never moving at over 30 miles per hour. He felt tired, dirty, and stressed. The pressure made him wonder why he was here. They had the technology, so a video conference was possible. In cases involving countries where movement is difficult for foreigners, he dealt with the entire incident from the safety of his headquarters.

He asked himself why he wanted to solve this case. His job involved offering a solution, but the final resolution belonged to the local police in Spain or abroad. There was always a handover. When the perpetrator was Spanish, the national police or the guardia dealt with the prosecution stages.

His team had missed crucial evidence and pride insisted that he put that right and because he liked Richard enough to call him a friend. This case was very personal for him. He sat in the slow traffic, tapping the steering wheel.

'What else? He asked himself. Why was he here? Thinking time adds value to a long journey because as he turned into his hotel, he realised two crucial things:

He didn't trust Jane Landis; someone had persuaded her to ignore evidence and misdirect him, either that or she helped instigate the whole thing. If we left it to her, we might never catch the real criminals.

The other reason was deeper. Galicia was his family home. He identified himself as Galician before Spanish and unsolved murder on the Camino hurt his homeland. This identity issue he linked with his personal battle between family and career. A battle his father had struggled with, moving to London to find work, only returning home when he retired. He had watched his father's struggle with his homesickness throughout his childhood. It was the story of Galicia itself.

His hotel, in contrast to his car, was well heated, comfortable and small. He avoided chain hotels when he could, and this was the accommodation he liked. He regarded his room with satisfaction, smallish but with a desk, a chair and a practical shower room. The furniture was oak and solid, with deep coloured fabrics and tasteful fittings and the service was discreet and prompt. It was not economic, but in central London even hostels aren't cheap and his expenses claim covered it.

Next, he needed to find where Richard was staying, and the hotel receptionist provided him with a local map. Of course, he had his phone, but you miss so much if you glue your eyes to a screen. He walked because he had spent enough time in his hire car today. And he wanted to experience the London of his youth, and the plan helped locate his old haunts. Tomorrow he planned to meet his friend, but this evening he had a chance for nostalgia.

A quick look at the map showed Richard was staying twenty minutes' walk away, and near a pub he used to visit. London had changed in ten years. His colleague was joining him for lunch, but not at the demolished Drake and Lion.

"OK," he laughed. "I'm in your hands. I will be there in twenty minutes."

'The smells of this city are distinct,' he thought as he walked, different from Madrid. The sky was grey and bleak, but the icy rain had stopped. London has something dark about it that the summer sun can't cure, and it intoxicated Miguel. He grew up here amid the noise and the bustle. And so many trees. He had forgotten how green the city was with its parks and gardens. By the time he reached Patricia's, he was enjoying the nostalgia. It was not a neighbourhood he remembered, but the place he loved lingered behind the multicultural food vans, cafes and takeaways, and the residential streets remained the same.

They ended up in an Italian bistro that Patricia recommended, and not a pub. It was dark inside, but it smelt of garlic and tomatoes and a hum of conversation provided background as people filled tables for the midday special. Over lunch, Richard told him what he recalled of the bombing. Information that worried Miguel.

"Do they know you have remembered the details?"

"I sent a copy of my notes to John, but I haven't discussed it with anyone else."

"Do you think it's possible that Chief Inspector Landis is part of this?"

Richard thought for a moment.

"I'm sure the team working with her noticed a problem. John has been feeding me information through this entire case and intimated that the squad was behind him. But he has been careful, always waiting till I asked and never badmouthing his boss."

"So they suspect foul play but need proof, or someone willing to stick their head above the parapet and make a complaint?"

"To be fair, I guess they hoped I would regain my memory and provide them with what they needed. It's not their fault I ignored the facts and wallowed in grief instead of looking for those responsible."

Miguel carried on, "What about Sir Giles? What do you think of his involvement?"

"I'm not sure, some kind of fall-guy, perhaps, but I am pretty positive that when he saw Molly's body, his grief was genuine, so I would guess he didn't kill her himself," said Richard.

"No, we are certain that was Geraldine. We found some evidence and managed at last to link it all together. But was he involved in what happened or even order her death? The letters came from his office with or without his knowledge."

"Do you know that for sure?"

"This case and finding out that much has exhausted the favours owed me. Only Jane can give more information and if she gets involved, we would lose our advantage. We could solve this in an afternoon if she arrested Geraldine, about whom we have sufficient proof to proceed. But then we wouldn't be certain if Chief Inspector Landis has tampered with evidence as part of the organisation."

"On a personal level, I want the person who killed Gill in prison, but also those responsible for the bombing and the officers who allowed them to escape justice. But you're interested in the bigger picture?" asked Richard.

"So, where do we go from here?"

"Geraldine has committed three murders. Would she talk if we arrested her?"

"She has acted as a professional assassin, so either she has murdered before, in which instance she won't talk. Or she has a personal motivation, in which case we need something as leverage. Also, she might disappear before we get to her."

"What about Jack? Why was he killed and what did Molly know about his identity?" asked Richard.

"The team has spoken to a witness who heard them arguing. Molly suspected her boyfriend was not who she had imagined. The row was genuine. Molly separated from Sally and Tom so that she could learn more about him, but jack was meeting someone in Portomarín and took a taxi."

"Dave Bromley, the sleuth, also heard them arguing, and claimed that Molly knew Jack was a detective. So they separated from their friends for another reason."

"I don't know what that changes. But it gives us two

diverse versions," said Miguel.

"Why was an undercover policeman there? Do we have that information?"

"Yes, he was part of the Sheffield anti-terrorist squad following Molly. She was a member of the same fascist group with which we associated the professor. After years of relative inactivity, they have recruited again. Not only that, but been involved in incidents all over Europe aimed at stirring up ill feeling toward immigrants.

Molly was meeting with the Neo-Nazi groups. The Camino, with its wide range of nationalities, provided cover for the meetings."

"Could it be that Jack was the intended target? If someone found out who he was," asked Richard.

"As far as we know, he had received what he thought were orders to meet someone in Portomarín. Jack wanted to leave in a taxi, but Molly needed to walk to get her Compostela, so they argued and split up," said Miguel.

"Were the orders genuine?"

"No, but they must have sounded very realistic and included a code word."

There were water damaged, mind-maps in Jack's pocket. They hinted at an attack on the Cathedral, to increase religious tensions."

"But now it looks as though her own group killed her?"

"Neither Tom nor Sally liked Jack, but they both thought that he and Molly were in love."

"Maybe they were. It's not unheard of."

"What if they were getting more serious, and Molly changed her mind? What if the Camino transformed her, and she wanted a path out?" asked Richard.

"The scenario fits, but few humans change. For a policeman, you are generous in your view of nature," said

Miguel.

"When I walked the Way, it resolved many things in my life. I met God and found a new relationship with my wife, so of course I believe lives can change. I have hope."

The colonel patted Richard's shoulder. "I envy your faith, a*migo*."

"The team has worked hard since I left. Come on, I'll introduce you to Patricia and come up with a plan of action over coffee," said Richard, moving them back onto safe ground.

They never got their coffee.

# CHAPTER TWENTY-FIVE

## *Richard has a problem*

They walked 500 metres, chatting, before a police car drew up alongside them and two plain-clothes officers got out. They walked round in front of Miguel and Richard, blocking their path. One of them spoke to Richard.

"Would you mind giving us your name, sir?"

"Richard Harris, can I help you?"

"Get in the car, please? We need to have a word."

"Is it about the joy rider who caused my accident?"

"No, it's more serious. We will explain everything at the station."

The posture of the men worried him because they stood so close, blocking his exit and trapping him between themselves and the vehicle and the driver, a uniformed constable, kept his hand on the door handle. Richard turned toward Miguel and one man grabbed his arm and then took his stick, forcing him to stagger and lean on the automobile for support. It was as if they expected him to run.

He gasped in shock before forcing a smile. "I didn't catch your name, nor that of your colleague," he said.

He hoped to remind them of protocol, but his awkward turn countered his authority.

However, the man flushed. "Sorry, sir. I'm Detective Sergeant Peter Morris, and this is Detective Sergeant John Hornman."

"Next, I'm going to ask my friend here to give a message to my landlady and then I'll be with you, Sergeant."

Richard kept his hand on the car as he turned slowly, hoping they gave him enough room to move.

"Perhaps you would explain the situation to Patricia, who has a gift for you, anyway. Also, depending on how long this takes, she may need to bring my medication to the police station. Which office will we be at?"

The sergeant supplied the details and relaxed, but Miguel tensed. Richard shook his head, hoping that his colleague kept quiet. An arrest was something he had foreseen as a possibility confirming Jane Landis' involvement.

There was no arrest yet, but the officers were giving every sign they planned to charge him upon their arrival. The best way for Jane Landis to neutralise his witness statement on the bombing was to discredit him, ensuring that his account was less valuable. He had predicted that when attempts at ending his life failed, his detention was Plan B. He hoped the colonel had noted the names of the detectives involved.

An officer helped him into the police car, and he watched through the window as Miguel got out his map and set off towards Patricia's house. It was up to Miguel whether the plan worked.

* * *

He hoped Patricia could open an investigation and get someone in his corner. She had everything on paper, and instructions on where to find evidence.

Richard tried to think logically about what he found.

At the museum, an explosive planted in a doorway caused his injury. He saw it being placed and who placed it but didn't realise, at the time, the importance of what he saw.

The bombers planned it for someone else, but when it exploded, it was him they wanted to kill, and the story of the detonator was an invention.

Bomb makers delivering their goods were the guys he caught, not the bombers themselves.

Now he remembered the suspicious conversations he overheard and recalled the professor paying the two men.

He remembered much more damning material, but had not yet linked it with evidence.

There were copies of what he had so far, for Miguel and his lawyer, a friend of Patricia's. Richard had spoken to her, paying a retainer for her services. Patricia put the same information on a pen drive and the password to his computer, which he expected the police to confiscate.

It would be easy for Jane Landis to plant evidence on his computer, but if honest officers looked at the machine first, and they found his own evidence, it might cast doubt on her motives. He tried to delay that possibility by hiding it and placing an old laptop of Patricia's in his room with his data on it.

At the station, he expected to be arrested for Molly's murder after several days of adverse publicity. As the murder was outside his house and he had links with Molly, they could draw the implication that he was carried out the museum bombing. So they either charged him or publicised the implication.

As he lived in Spain, he was a flight risk, so likely to be remanded in custody somewhere, where, as an ex-police officer, he would be in danger.

Sitting in the car going over the possibilities, it surprised him they hadn't handcuffed him or pushed him around more. Adding resisting arrest to the other charges would further damage his reputation. Of course now you couldn't beat out a confession with a truncheon. But reasonable force was acceptable, showing who was the boss if a criminal resisted capture.

He was worried he had not done enough to protect himself, not sure that it was possible to avoid this.

He tried to breathe steadily.

The two police officers remained quiet in the car. He expected them to chat to get him to talk, a well-used method of obtaining useful information, but they said nothing, not even to the uniformed constable driving.

He wondered why they came with a driver. Was he a witness or extra muscle?

Sergeant Morris had taken his stick while he was talking to Miguel. But Richard noted his surprise when he stumbled and needed to use the car for support. The officers didn't know he had a disability.

Sergeant Morris gave it back when they reached the station so that he could walk to the interview room, but moved it out of his reach when he sat down.

They gave him a cup of tea and then left him alone with an officer outside the door and a camera in the corner, recording his movements.

The experience was deliberately nerve-wracking and not knowing what they might ask, or charge him with, and the lack of control was frightening. Indeed, having his stick put out of reach was demeaning. Sure, it was against regulations because he had a registered disability, but they insisted it was a weapon, not a walking aid. Taking a deep breath, he tried to marshal his thoughts.

The interview was likely to follow protocol even if they intended to bend the system, and he was aware of how bendable it was. Good detectives, when they were up against it, pushed hard. So his experience was the structure could be bent and stay credible and legitimate. Still, his knowledge of the organisation was some protection. The most crooked of police teams contained honest officers, so he needed to find them and get them on his side.

# CHAPTER TWENTY-SIX

## *Miguel's plan*

An hour after they detained Richard, Patricia was pacing in the drawing room of her house while Miguel explained what had happened.

"I didn't believe him when he told me being arrested was a possibility," she said.

He stood with his rear to the fireplace, and she looked at him directly.

"Where do you stand? Are you working with me, or do you regard Richard as a suspect?"

She sounded fierce, and he took a step back, stumbling on the hearth.

"No, he is not a suspect. He has an alibi. We checked that first. Anyway, there is sufficient evidence to arrest someone else, and that's why I came. I was going to see Chief Inspector Landis after I heard about it. This development has shocked me, but now we get him back here.."

"Good, I'll make us a coffee and then we can start," said

Patricia.

Her enthusiasm encouraged Miguel, who was glad that Richard's friends were so loyal.

"Richard claimed that you have a gift for me and I guessed that this 'gift' might prove important."

She put her coffee on the table and left, returning with a large brown envelope.

"He meant this, a record of everything he remembered happening at the London museum, a plan and some of our findings and suppositions about the Westminster Exhibition. Information from the anti-terror squad in Sheffield and a few more bits and pieces about Lord Bonham and Sir Giles. A statement and sketch from a private detective and some material on the IRA. I don't remember if there is anything else."

"He put this together in two days!"

"Not much sleep!"

"Look, I had better ring Julia. She is a lawyer and a friend, and she already knows she might be called upon," said Patricia.

Miguel opened the envelope, but he could hear snatches of the conversation. "No, it's not a favour. You'll get paid over and above the retainer that we left for you. Absolutely, it is urgent…... Police corruption…... a peer of the realm... a knighted MP……. Yes, that police officer ... No, I don't suppose it will be easy. Thanks, I know I owe you big time."

Miguel grinned. "No mention of Spanish law enforcement?"

"No point in telling her everything. She needs some surprises. How else is she going to earn her fee? Besides, it sounds bad enough without mentioning it's also an international incident."

"How good is she? It could be difficult if corruption is involved."

"Don't worry about that, because she is at her best in complex situations. When she has seen Richard, she'll phone and hopefully bring him back here this afternoon."

Miguel thought it unlikely, but didn't say so.

"Let me take this to my hotel to study it because I because I need to talk to my team to get a grip on this. Also, it looks as though I can't trust Chief Inspector Landis and we need someone here we can talk to. Could we exchange telephone numbers and keep in touch?"

Once at his hotel, he immediately got to work.

The envelope contained a letter.

*Dear Miguel,*

*I fear I'm in grave danger; I've remembered what happened on the night my wife died and collected evidence to support what I remember.*

*It is here in this pouch, together with the information we uncovered regarding the Westminster Exhibition. Patricia has a copy. I hope against hope that I can count both of you as friends and allies in this matter.*

*I am giving you this in case of another attempt on my life.*

*Jane might arrest me to discredit any testimony I give about the bombing (John has a copy of my statement, his number is 020\*\*\*\*\*\*\*,) as I know that Jane Landis manipulated the evidence in the original case, and so we can't trust her. The proof is on the pen drive included. The sources of the information are anonymous for the moment as people risked their jobs to help me get this and, if it becomes public knowledge too soon, may risk their lives. I have safeguarded their identities and taken statements from those willing to speak out in a trial.*

*We have everything we need to make arrests. Doing that, with*

*Chief Inspector Landis in charge of the Molly Hambleton Murder, is going to prove very difficult. My advice is to start in Sheffield. If something happens to me, then Tom Miller may well be in danger.*

*However, it remains your case. I hope this helps.*

*Richard.*

Miguel emptied the envelope, switched on his computer, and worked. He had an urgent phone call from Manuel in Spain, who told him that a British police officer had arrived and insisted on a search of Richard's house and his laptop taking paperwork as evidence.

They wiped everything in the drawer, even the papers. After the break-in, we fingerprinted anywhere that looked disturbed and photographed it, intending to check with Richard for missing items, although we never did that. Is it possible the break-in was to plant something? We wouldn't know about it if we hadn't been using the gallery. There is a formal request for the physical evidence we hold. It's logged and photographed. Do I hand it to them?"

"Yes, there's no choice. Make sure you take photos and copies of the lot. List everything and require him to sign the list. Nothing must go missing."

That took Manuel aback. "Why would it get lost? I wanted to give you more time. Things were hastening, and he hadn't communicated Jane's probable involvement to his team."

"Tonight, there will be more to say."

"Oh, and the general called very unhappy, he says, that you have switched your phone off, and he needs to talk to you ASAP."

Miguel cringed. "Did you tell him where I was?"

"No choice, boss, sorry."

"OK, my mobile will be off for the next two hours at least. After that, I hope to tell him I have evidence.

"Understood," said Manuel.

So he rang off, promising to update them when he could.

London was never quiet despite the hotel being in a back street. There is traffic, and communities, and birdsong, the sounds of his childhood. It was so different to Madrid. The familiarity reassured him as he sat thinking and, for a moment, he was uncertain because he was a team player. Working best when his squad was together and he could use their resources and skills to enhance his own. His strength was in being an excellent leader, bringing out the finest in colleagues. But, his weakness was when acting alone with no one to bounce his ideas from or dismiss the doubts he made mistakes. He didn't have the initiative or self-assurance that he had seen in Richard.

Then he read Richard's letter again and noticed John's number; he phoned it. When he introduced himself, John's voice became cautious.

"I'm at work, but the shift finishes at eight. How about we meet for a drink in the Red Lion on Burley Street?"

Miguel said nothing but John continued, " yes, brilliant, we've a bit of catching up to do. See you later."

The officer was obviously unable to talk.

With two hours' spare, he checked everything he knew, and that Richard had left.


The Red Lion was dark, old-fashioned stained glass windows and maroon velvet upholstery, caused it to feel even darker. As it was Monday evening, it was quiet and Miguel breathed in the combined aromas of stale beer, sweat and food, that make the atmosphere in a traditional

London pub unique. Behind the main tap room was a maze of smaller rooms. A few men clustered round the bar, which ran the length of the building with booths under the front windows and an open floor space at one end, where it turned a corner. A square bar ran through smaller rooms, which had tables and chairs, not booths and were quieter, with more space. His eyes were adjusting when a tap on his shoulder got his attention. John introduced his companion as Inspector Davis of administration and statistics.

"The chief inspector at the time transferred me to admin and stats after I asked questions about the evidence sent to the CPS. They were hoping I'd resign. But SHE was given a promotion," said Davis.

John was eager to say something: "To be safe from more questions, they broke up the entire team investigating the bombing immediately after the investigation closed. It was then that I requested a transfer to Landis's new squad, hoping I could find indications of corruption."

"I told him what happens in a shit hole is that you get covered in shit," said Davis.

"She's Teflon-coated. Everyone thinks she's the face of modern policing."

"Did anyone else have doubts?" asked Miguel.

"Two other officers, but they're not willing to identify themselves unless we prove something."

The colonel nodded, aware that whistle blowers had a habit of losing everything.

"Any senior officers?"

"The super in our division is a slimy git and thinks that the sun shines out of her backside," said John with more emotion than Miguel expected.

Davis paused. "My chief superintendent is pretty anti-corruption. Some say he's anal about it. when I joined the division, he made a point of telling me. He might know who to talk to. Have we got anything concrete, though? We hoped DCI Harris's statement would open a review but, well, mud sticks."

"Yes, I think we have enough, but time is not on our side. If we pulled together a team to go through evidence and build a file, I could take it to your chief super, away from Jane Landis, and make it official. A complaint from a senior officer on an overseas force would be at least treated seriously."

The two men looked at each other. To talk about it is easy, but taking action and putting your job, pension and reputation on the line is hard.

"I'm in. I've already talked to the wife, who reckons there's nothing more evil than a bent copper."

Davis nodded. "Yes, I'm in. The bombing case left a nasty taste in my mouth and I wished I'd shouted louder."

Miguel contacted Patricia to check they could use her house, and they decided to start at eight the following morning and settled down to finish their drink.

But Patricia rang back, suggesting they come at once, as Julia had returned from seeing Richard.

With a glance at his co-conspirator.

"Might as well get started, I'll just phone the wife." said Davis.

John nodded and Miguel informed Patricia that they were on their way.

# CHAPTER TWENTY-SEVEN

## In custody earlier that day

*Earlier that day.*

An hour later, Richard sat alone in a small square room for an hour. Although he had been in interview rooms before, they never seemed so bare with the smell of sweat and disinfectant so noticeable. And the peeling paint that ran round the skirting boards made him wonder about the state of the building. The wait made him nervous, and he wondered why they hadn't arrested him already. He breathed deeply, forcing himself to relax and give them nothing to look at.

Some are better than others at psychological games and at this moment he wished he had not dismissed such games, snobbishly thinking of them as dishonest because now he forced to play against Jane, who excelled. He would need to learn if he was going to enter the world of international crime. For a while, he doubted his ability to cope, but after a time, he simply sat. Even nervous, he was patient. Someone would come eventually and waiting must not affect him.

In Spain, the chief inspector had referred to his disability and before she did, he hadn't realised how sensitive he was. So her constant reference to things he couldn't do rattled him, but he wouldn't allow her to intimidate him by using the same references again.

At last, Jane entered the room with Sergeant Morris.

"My apology for keeping you waiting, Richard," she said, smiling and sitting down. He smiled, aware she wasn't sorry.

After she sat down, she showed they were being filmed and gave everyone's name, including Richard's, and other than agreeing he was called Richard Harris, he kept quiet.

Was it time for his lawyer to be involved? There was no guarantee he could survive this ordeal, and gruesome stories heard from ex-coppers behind bars played in his mind.

"The sergeant here says being brought in didn't surprise you."

A quick glance at Peter Morris caught bewilderment in his eyes, but even if the officer hadn't said it, it was accurate.

"So perhaps you could save some time and tell us why you killed Molly Hardcastle. I can make a guess, but I would prefer it in your own words."

The announcement shook him because he had expected days of trying to get him to incriminate himself, suggestions that he was part of a criminal group, all kinds of possibilities that would discredit him, but not this direct attack.

"Now, I want a lawyer." he said.

"I thought I would give you a chance, as a friend, to explain why you killed Molly and your wife before I arrested you. A guilty plea and confession would have helped you."

That stunned Richard because Jane had added the words 'your wife' so quietly and unexpectedly that for a minute it didn't register and then, when it did, his world collapsed. They were accusing him of killing Gill. He tried without success to keep his breathing even, but he could not cope. Panic started in his stomach and rose into his chest, and his eyes blurred. They would go over the detail many times and force him to re-live it all. It was going to break him. It was designed to break him.

Jane caught the panic as he watched the triumph in her expression. She was putting her papers back into their paper cover.

"Could you book him in and contact his lawyer?" she said to Sergeant Morris. She waited until they had cautioned Richard, then ended the interview and left without another word. He was familiar with the process, but the humiliation was excruciating, and he would be glad when he reached a cell and was alone with his thoughts. He was sure they would make him wait as long as possible before they questioned him again because they wanted to break him and they were close.

His familiarity with the booking process had at least forced him to breathe more slowly. The sergeant removed his stick along with the contents of his pockets and he hung onto the edge of the counter. When he picked up the pen to sign the docket, it forced him to lean heavily forwards.

"Stand back Mr Harris, you should know better than that."

Without thinking, and in response to the tone, he moved backwards and his leg buckled under him and he hit the tiled floor hard, winding him.

Both the sergeants stood over him as he recovered enough to speak.

"Sorry, I can't balance without sticks."

There was no response, but his voice was weak, his breathing not yet normal. He felt the tiles beneath his cheek gritty, having last been cleaned hours ago. He contemplated staying, closing his eyes as though the world didn't exist.

"You will need to help me up."

His voice was stronger this time as he pronounced each word separately. If there was no response, he would close his eyes and wait. If they called the doctor, at least that would confirm that he needed a stick.

At last they sprang into action, and manoeuvred him into a cell, where he collapsed onto the bed, overcome with both pain and humiliation.

He could push up into a sitting position after a few minutes.

When he arrived, he thought maybe they were scaring and discrediting him to keep him away from the investigation. After all, what evidence could there be? Unless they had planted something that would convict him of one or more murders. Or were they trying to twist the facts to fit and basing a case on circumstances? It depended on how far Jane Landis was prepared to go, how deep her involvement was and how corrupt she had become. At the moment, she had the odds in her favour whichever route she took.

He sat and waited, time passing slowly, but somewhere close by a church clock marked the hours, so at least he knew how long he had been there. The duty sergeant brought him sandwiches for dinner with a mug of tea, then hesitated, hovering in the doorway.

"I have added a note in the records stating you need a stick to walk. I was told to log it as a weapon, but I'll return it in the morning. And I'll ensure that you meet with your counsel, despite the chief inspector."

"Thank-you, I appreciate that."

He decided not to ask questions and at 10 pm, his lawyer arrived.

She was a woman of his own age who regarded him thoughtfully, absorbing every detail.

"Julia Downey, and don't get up. I know about your leg," she said. Her voice was deep and even. She was holding out her hand, which Richard shook. Her grip was firm and businesslike, belying her appearance, which was wild. Blond curls bursting out of a bun and a crinkled shirt escaping from a crinkled skirt.

"Sorry it's so late. I've been trying to get to see you since lunchtime. You must have upset someone influential, because climbing Everest would have been easier than getting in here. First, they said that you hadn't requested representation, then that they hadn't charged you, then the duty sergeant was busy and goodness knows what else. I can be quite persistent, though. We haven't been given much time and they plan to question you in the morning." She stopped to take a breath.

"What have they charged you with, or are the charges being brought tomorrow?"

"Two counts of murder and obstructing a police investigation. They cautioned me, but official charges with you there." He avoided saying out loud, who they accused him of murdering. He still felt raw and very vulnerable.

"Good, that's what they told me. Did they say anything else?"

"They asked for a confession," He was finding it hard to speak and therefore it was easier to be brief.

Julia looked at him and seemed to realise his emotional state.

"You hadn't expected them to accuse you of murdering your wife?"

He shook his head.

"Patricia gave me a brief rundown on the phone, but I haven't yet seen the packet of information that you prepared for me. I will have by the morning."

There was a knock. It was the officer.

"I am going off duty, and the chief inspector says that Miss Downey has to leave before changeover, and she's already angry that I let you in here tonight, Miss."

"Five minutes. I promise I won't get you into trouble." The door closed again, but Richard could hear the sergeant outside.

"I'm off to Patricia's. Don't offer them anything, and we'll deal with the rest tomorrow."

Patricia had assured him that Julia excelled at her job, but she didn't look fierce enough. People made the same mistake about him and he knew it was best not to judge, but he was tired and nervous and he hadn't got his painkillers, so his hip ached; he was emotional and feeling very low. At least she was on his side.

The new duty sergeant opened the door and surprised him.

"Bill, I wondered when I would see someone who knew me."

"Chief Inspector Harris, I don't believe it!"

"You mean rumours of this aren't circulating round the Met?"

"I heard that an ex-copper was in for questioning. I

would never guess it would be you, though."

"And yet here I am." Richard leaned against the wall, too weary to hide his exhaustion.

The veteran officer hesitated in the doorway. "Can I get you anything?"

Richard shook his head.

"I'll leave you to it then," he paused.

"I'll do everything in my power to help. You count on that."

"You haven't asked if I'm guilty," said Richard, looking directly at Bill.

"No need is there, sir?"

"Just Richard these days, sergeant, and thank you."

# CHAPTER TWENTY-EIGHT

## *Patricia's house*

That evening Patricia ordered take-away food, which they ate in the kitchen. Miguel explained what evidence he and his team had, and how it tied in with the statement from Richard. He had left his laptop and the paper file in the hotel safe, but he promised them copies of everything the next day. They finished and when the lawyer arrived, moved to Patricia's sitting room.

Julia, the solicitor, spoke first. "Richard is pretty shaken. Chief Inspector Landis has told him they will charge him with the murder of his wife, Molly Hardcastle, interfering with a police inquiry and obstruction of justice."

There was silence for a few minutes.

"My God," said John.

She had more to say.

"However, I think there is a problem because I tried to see him all afternoon and they offered me excuse after excuse. Not legal, of course, but hard to prove its deliberate obstruction. Meanwhile, they were trying to push him into a confession. I chatted with him briefly in the cells. I think they know he's not guilty. If the accusation sticks, even if it's dismissed later, it makes his statement inadmissible in court and discredits everything he says."

"Why didn't they charge him today?" asked Patricia.

"Either wasting time or waiting for something."

"What would she be waiting for?"

"Jane sent an officer to Spain to search his house and collect the physical evidence from the murders of Molly and Jack. He flies back in the morning. My team phoned me earlier to tell me about it."

"What were they searching for?" asked Julia.

"I don't know, but someone broke into his house while he was at the guardia barracks. Nothing was missing, but my squad is now wondering if they added something."

"DCI Landis falsified evidence in the bombing case to get those two guys convicted of murder and planting a bomb, but I found no proof because she covered her tracks well." Davis sounded defeated.

"She may have given information to the press and is waiting to see what comes of it."

"How do you mean?"

Julia looked at them. "Is there any truth in their accusations? Is it possible he killed his wife?

There was quiet. No one wanted to answer that question.

Miguel was the first to speak. "We need to deal with facts. There is no chance he killed Molly. He has a solid alibi. It's the first thing we checked, but he could have murdered Jack. We didn't check if Richard had an alibi for that."

John said, "He couldn't have hurt his wife. The

explosion injured him before she died, but the DCI signed off on all the evidence herself, and the medical examiner is famous for submitting his reports in bad handwriting, which some poor sod has to type up."

"How can you be sure?"

"I was there. The uniform guys called me because Inspector Davis was on duty and they couldn't get hold of him. DI Landis, Sergeant Munro and the DI arrived together. Mrs Harris was with paramedics by then. I accompanied DCI Harris to hospital and was just leaving when everyone else reported in."

Davis looked at him. "I didn't realise that."

"Does that mean that Jane Landis isn't aware of that?" asked Julia.

"I couldn't say, but I don't recall ever talking to her about it."

Miguel shifted in his seat. John wasn't much of a talker, and Jane treated her sergeants as servants or organisational tools. But if she didn't know, it would be shoddy police work. But Davis hadn't known either, so perhaps she didn't.

"Who recounted events to you?" he asked Davis.

"Someone called Lord Bonham. He organised the exhibition. He saw the whole thing. The uniform guys got there, but they handed the scene to the bomb squad until they could declare it safe. They had just let the ambulance crews through as I arrived.

They needed to get the chief inspector out of there as his condition was precarious and they were trying to resuscitate Mrs Harris, but they pronounced her dead at the scene."

"So, what do we do now? Does Julia tell them all this?

We need to know how deep the rot goes. It won't hurt

Richard to spend one night in the cells. In the meantime, we talk to someone honest."

They were still in the sitting room. The colonel thought ending this and getting Richard back should be easier but something important was hovering on the edge of his vision. They had outsmarted him, so he was always behind and now when he needed the complete picture he was running out of time.

"The group will scatter when they realise how much evidence we have," said Davis with obvious pleasure.

"Are we sure we have the ringleader?" inquired Julia, who was weighing the chances of this going to court.

"No, I guess that's Sutherland, but he has more or less kept his hands clean."

"What about Sir Giles? I have met him, and whereas I don't like the guy, he always appears to be more hot air than substance."

"Someone convinced him he was the victim of the bombing. Whether Molly was callous enough to kill her own father is another matter. But he is a genuine member of the real IRA as in the Russia, Iran, Business Association. RIBA because it's a business oriented group, he didn't associate them with the death threats. Whoever dreamt up the plan was too subtle for Sir Giles and some other MPs. The purpose of the genuine RIBA is to bring about trading agreements between Russia, Iran and the West, which would have aided peace in the Middle East. Lord Bonham started dropping the B for Business to make them sound more like terrorists. He also changed the order of the initials because the British public already associates the initials IRA with terrorism."

"I haven't yet seen the point of anything that

happened," admitted John.

"It's complicated, and we need Richard to explain the whole thing. Remember that fascists are not a unified group, nor are they terrorists. Their purpose is to bring a country together under a single flag and one leader, opposed to democracy, but with no qualms about using it when it suits them. And, they believe that violent action is a unifying force. Attacking foreigners and the weak or different is another way to achieve that end.

The reason they planned bombings was to stir up hate against Muslims, then designing the bombs to damage the museum building with minimum injuries."

Each person had only seen one puzzle piece, and now saw a conspiracy involving members of Parliament, Police, and Peers of the Realm. They were hoping beyond hope it wasn't even more widespread.

Julia, whose prime concern was Richard, spoke.

"OK, about Richard's release, you don't want me to disclose anything. So could I have alternative suggestions, please?"

"We haven't sorted out the evidence. It may take a while."

"Is your chief super in the office this week? He isn't at a conference or on holiday," said Miguel.

"There is a protocol meeting with him tomorrow afternoon, so I guess he is around."

"What time does his PA arrive?"

"Eight o'clock."

"Right, give me the number of your duty officer and five minutes," said Miguel.

Both he and the General reported to the Chief Justice in Spain. Ranks in the guardia do not equate well to British police, but he knew if he used his rank, they were bound to listen. He phoned his boss, the general, to explain. Dealing with corruption in another country's law enforcement was significant enough to call for it. It was a delicate political situation.

The call took longer than the five minutes he had promised. The chief didn't like being disturbed at a dinner party. However, he understood the position at once and grasped the diplomatic problems and the danger of an international incident.

"Don't talk to anyone. You know what might happen. I am going to get the British Police commissioner out of bed. How high do you think the corruption goes?"

"Maybe the chief superintendent, but we're not sure, sir."

"Well, finding out is their problem, not mine. There had better be solid evidence against Jane Landis?"

"Oh yes. More than anyone else, in fact."

"This will do nothing for our relationship with the UK and they'll hate us for catching them out?"

"But we can't just ignore it, sir?"

"No, and your job is to establish the information is strong. And don't mess around with your murder inquiry or anything, do you understand? That is no longer your headache. I will ensure the release of your friend in the morning. But collect your proof together and the rest is their problem."

The colonel was holding his phone away from his ear because the chief had finished his meal with a couple of brandies, and it was making him very emphatic.

The phone went dead long before Miguel responded.

When he walked into the sitting room, everyone looked shattered.

"Sorry to be so long. Julia, they won't get an extension

on the twenty-four-hour holding period and they will need one if they are waiting for the officer sent to Galicia to return. I can't tell you more because my chief is getting your commissioner out of bed and he will take over. He will need that evidence.

After that, he leaned against the wall in exhaustion. He had nothing left to give, and he was too emotionally involved.

# CHAPTER TWENTY-NINE

*The following morning and the plan unfolds*

Later, Richard went through events once again. It was strange that Sergeant Bill Riley was the first person who knew him. He had spent his entire career in London. He recognised almost everyone by sight, but Jane must have found officers who had never met him deliberately. She didn't want friendly faces there until he incriminated himself. They didn't need to be dishonest, just not question what she was doing.

Bill's support gave him hope, and he dozed off into a troubled sleep full of muddled images of Gill, with Molly standing over her, Geraldine and Sir Giles laughing by his bedside, the professor lurking in a narrow alley, the light behind him, giving him a fiendish appearance. He woke up at once. The strange dream reminded him of Sally's murder in Sheffield. Tom recognised the suspects.

If Jane was given their names and linked them to the professor's group, Tom's life was in danger because he could identify the group and she was bound to pass that information on to Lord Bonham. He didn't know what to do. If Bill inquired, she would find out.

Another troubling idea came to him. What if his friend believed he was guilty? The obvious first suspect is the person who finds the body. Molly was outside his house, after all.

The dream exhausted him. Enough to fall back to sleep, but still, his thoughts haunted him.

The sergeant woke him with a mug of tea and toast.

"Rumour has it that DCI Landis wants you sitting in an interview room for a couple of hours before your brief arrives. She has already given Peter Morris an earful for not charging you with resisting arrest."

"I didn't resist, and he didn't arrest me."

"That's what he says to the chief inspector. But she said you were dangerous and they should have cuffed you anyway, and we should count your stick as a weapon and log it. "

"You realise I can't walk without it?"

"Yes sir, Steve Menis, the day sergeant, told me you needed help to get to the cell. So as a precaution, the duty doctor's coming. Now I've seen 'the lie of the land' like."

He stopped by the door.

"One thing, Peter Morris is honest, under the thumb, but solid. John Hornman is very young and keen, a fast-track type and eager to impress. There'll be others, though."

No need for him to finish. Some police worked well and others didn't.

In a hierarchical organisation, it is difficult to disobey a senior leader because it affects your chance of promotion, so few take the risk.

The doctor agreed that Richard's stick was essential for mobility and, after phoning the hospital, insisted that they sent for his medication, and this thwarted Jane's plan.

Richard heard the argument between the sergeant and John Hornman, the officer sent to arrest him.

"The doc is with him and he stays here till he's finished."

"Why the bloody hell is the doctor here, Bill? There was nothing wrong last night."

"'Cos he's disabled. He was in a car accident and is under a hospital specialist. I was told, under no circumstances was he allowed his stick, and yet I found he can't walk without it."

The conversation paused, and Richard wondered if the young detective was weighing up the older man's words.

"Go on, sergeant, he's putting one over on you, an ex-copper who knows the system. The boss says he's as crooked as they come."

"I'm not risking it, mate. I'm going by the book while he's in my care. If I were you, I'd make a few phone calls before you decide he's bent."

"A crony of his, are you?"

"Look lad, I've being doing this job since before you were born. You better learn not to believe anything without checking. You can't have him till the doc says so because this is not the Wild West." Bill banged his fist on the counter and that ended the conversation.

The doctor was asking Richard what his medication was and taking notes, forcing his concentration back to the present.

When John Hornman reappeared an hour later and unlocked Richard's cell, he had lost his cocky air. He handed him his stick without comment and escorted him to the interview room in silence, and gave him a drink, but he didn't know if the younger man had taken Bill's advice.

"I'll tell the chief inspector we're ready," was what he said. But Richard hadn't finished the tea before he and Jane were back, with his solicitor in tow. She had lost the rumpled, frustrated look of the previous evening and he couldn't read her expression.

After the introductions, Julia spoke first. "Before we waste time trying to intimidate my client into confessing to something he didn't do, I want to see your evidence. Otherwise, I suggest that we all go home."

She leaned back in her chair, looking relaxed.

"Oh yes, we have a witness who says that you were in the right place to kill your wife, but that she called out your name when you stabbed her to tell everyone who killed her.

There is paperwork suggesting that you knew that Molly Hambleton was on the Camino, and that she was blackmailing you because she saw you killing your wife."

Richard opened his mouth to speak, but Julia spoke first.

"Where is the proof for these charges?"

"The paperwork is on the way from Spain," replied Jane.

"Is this paper work coming by carrier pigeon? Does the Spanish police force not use modern technology?"

"Someone is collecting it in person." The DCI looked less comfortable now.

"In that case, you have nothing to back up those charges, Chief Inspector. I can see no reason to keep him here, so we're leaving. Phone us when your 'someone' arrives with something more concrete."

"Not possible. Your client is certain to leave the country."

"If you won't take his word, he will be happy to

surrender his passport until we sort this out. In fact, I brought it with me."

There was a knock. "Ma'am?"

"Can it wait?" said Jane.

"No, ma'am. The super wants a word."

The DCI left the room.

Julia winked at him while Sergeant Hornman remained quiet.

When she returned, she did not look happy. Whatever the super had suggested, she hadn't liked it. She took the passport and handed Richard a receipt that they both signed and asked John to escort them out.

When they reached the door, detective Hornman spoke.

"Take care, sir. We'll let you know if we receive some evidence." There was an emphasis on 'if'.


Late the previous evening, when Miguel had left Patricia's, he had another phone call in the taxi.

"Colonel López-López?" a very cultured English voice asked. "Could I trouble you to come to my office at eight am?" There was no introduction, apology, or details. It was a command.

"Certainly, sir," he said, mimicking the politeness and cordiality in the tone. He realised then that he should have gone to the top from the start. Yet another mistake.

At seven thirty the next day, he walked up the stairs to the commissioner's office. They had shown him the lift, but he needed the thinking time that climbing stairs offered.

"Good morning, sir. As you are early, can I get you a coffee while you wait?"

Nobody got this far without an invitation. The PA was as commanding as her boss and she showed him to a comfortable settee in the corner of the large, light-filled office, resembling an ivory tower. Miguel was aware this was an illusion. Impressing those needing it, so the commissioner could be gracious.

He felt foolish not going to the top earlier. The chief was right to reprimand him. He had been in his current rank for six months. And he had spent most of his time pretending he could do it and not give up fieldwork because he enjoyed operational policing. Hence, because of the attraction of being part of a close-knit team, he had dropped the ball.

He had just started his coffee when the PA came to usher him into the commissioner's office. They were both imposing, and Miguel felt scruffy in comparison as he held out his hand.

"Thank you for seeing me, sir, and my apologies for not being in uniform. My visit to the UK was personal."

The seriousness of the case didn't mean that they skipped the pleasantries, and it was five minutes before the commissioner mentioned the matter.

"This is a very serious affair, colonel. I only wish you had come to me sooner."

"Again, I'm sorry, sir. I was hoping for something more concrete before I acted. When things happen that destroy careers and reputations, I prefer to be sure, but on reflection, I should have raised it earlier."

"Well, we need a plan of action. I admired the way you dealt with Egypt and Germany, so I know you have the experience. So, give me a summary of what you've found and your thoughts on the matter."

The commissioner moved over to the comfortable seating arrangement, motioning him to follow. The PA brought in coffee, fruit juice and baked goods.

The colonel realised he was putting the entire case into the commissioner's control.

Miguel was glad that he had lived in London because otherwise the meeting might have perplexed him. Politeness, which emphasised rank, was a British speciality he remembered. The breakfast, the civility, the enquiries about his family's health all pointed to the commissioner's power.

This happened in Spain, but afterwards, in celebrating a successful completion of an investigation.

"I'd like the complete story," the commissioner was saying. "Of course, our internal inquiry team will uncover and deal with any wrongdoing on the part of our officers. What I want is the background. Start at the beginning. I would love to know why you became involved. I understand that it's not in your normal remit."

As Miguel told the tale, he saw, once again, where he had gone wrong. There is nothing as good as hindsight to show your errors. He got in the way because he wasn't doing his job. Leaving no one to have an overview. Manuel could not lead the team and it was his fault they had missed things.

When he finished the narrative, he planned to make sure the investigation had the facilities needed.

The commissioner was a good listener. He allowed him to finish his story with only the occasional "I understand" and nod of the head.

"Lord Bonham has come to our attention before, but his wealth and position have protected him. I would like to see that end. Do you consider him the author of this situation?"

It has been difficult to find hard evidence.

"My gut feeling is that we clear this matter up before internal affairs take over. Do you concur?"

"May I offer a suggestion, sir? There is an unofficial unit meeting to collate material as we speak: Make that team official and then let the Sheffield anti-terror squad deal with the clean up."

"Some detectives you alluded to who suspected corruption and got shut down. Can you assure them there will be no penalty for speaking out?"

" Which departments do they work for?"

It was time to mention the officers' names and trust the commissioner.

"Inspector Davis works for admin and information and he suggested yesterday that I could talk to his chief superintendent, who stamps on any sign of corruption."

The Commissioner was nodding. "Yes, both those departments have enough separation not to alert DCI Landis. I'll make sure they know not to consult with her.

That we silenced protests suggests higher-ranking officers, so we have to work fast.

When they hear, the media will have a field day prompting questions in parliament. If you please excuse my language, I'd prefer the shit hit the fan later rather than sooner, so could I prevail on you to keep quiet for the time being?"

"The success of my job depends on my maintaining a good relationship with my overseas colleagues, and that relationship must prevail: despite the political climate, it suits us both to be discreet, I think."

The commissioner looked relieved.

"Then might I suggest you make your visit official and we establish this as a joint operation?"

The PA peered around the door.

"Sorry to interrupt, sir, but I was sure you would want these."

In her hand was a bundle of morning newspapers.

"Discretion is not a priority for everyone."

Miguel glanced at Richard's photo alongside a variety of sensational headlines.

"Not when publicity achieves more than truth."

The commissioner stood and shook his hand to make phone calls, and the colonel left to report back home and get his uniform shipped to him. First, he planned to talk to his boss and admit his mistakes. A conversation he dreaded. Then he needed to apologise to Manuel for his interference.

He exited the commissioner's splendid glass office, feeling lighter. The UK police force would complete the investigation.

As he was staying at their invitation, he planned to clean up mistakes made because he allowed himself to be influenced by corrupt officers.

# CHAPTER THIRTY

*Released for now*

An hour later, Richard leaned back against the taxi headrest, feeling weary. Although it was not yet lunchtime, he longed to go to bed and sleep. However, even though he was home, he was aware it wasn't finished, and the uncertainty frightened him.

His solicitor was with him, having parked at Patricia's house and taken a black cab to police headquarters, because the two public slots at the station were always full. They knew Patricia was bound to want any news they had.

Julia had told him about the work party, and he felt torn. Of course, he wished to join in because his own freedom was at stake. For now, he needed a shower, decent coffee, and a quiet hour before facing the world. He wanted no more surprises.

Julia's voice startled him.

"The house looks quiet." The taxi was at the door.

"The dining room is in the basement and I imagine they

preferred to use the table. We can let ourselves in with my key."

There was no response when he rang the bell and downstairs the basement was dark, and although there were several dirty coffee cups on the kitchen counter, no one was there. They were unsure of what to do.

"Right, I'll phone Miguel and you contact Patricia," said Richard.

So far, he and Julia hadn't talked about what happened next. They had expected to return to an investigation which would decide that for them. This was strange, and his anxiety returned.

Miguel's mobile was on voice mail, and he stumbled over the message.

"Phone me later. I'm back at Patricia's." It seemed inadequate.

Julia had more success with her call.

"She will arrive in half an hour. Put the coffee on. No, on second thoughts I'll do that. You take a shower and change because you look as though you've spent the night in a police cell. Whatever Patricia is going to tell us can wait until afterwards. Getting you home worked better than I expected. Since they had charged you, I was expecting a magistrate's hearing."

"Am I still paying for your time?"

The prospect of a shower and coffee had cheered him up and he was teasing her.

"Go, or I'll start charging double," she said, pointing at the door.

So, he left, realising as he did, he liked her even though he knew nothing about her, but he'd like her as a friend. But gratitude and exhaustion change your view of people.

So, he ran a bath, needing the passive warmth that a

tub provides to work through his turmoil and ease the ache in his hip. By the time he finished, he hoped that Julia would have explained everything to Patricia. The strange thing was, the warm water made him relax physically, but his mind was weary. The stress of the arrest and an inability to express the emotion he was feeling created the illusion that they had trapped him. Especially as it might all happen again.

When Patricia arrived with news that nothing more was happening today and that the police commissioner had taken the case, it was a relief. The newspapers with their embarrassing headlines were in her hand. The investigation was over for him. That should have given him a respite, but lack of control frustrated him. Mostly he worried they might arrest him again, as she had clarified that they would not investigate corruption charges until they had rounded up the members of the far right group. The newspapers added even more worry: 'Hero detective disgraced and arrested for murder' was the headline of one prominent paper. The papers carried his photo on their front page and as they sat at the kitchen table and ate bread and cheese, trying to decide the next move, he wondered if Jane had won.

"The chief superintendent suggested that there would be nothing to report today."

"If CS Bolin is in charge, it will be weeks, because I have never met a more retentive, nit picking, bureaucratic..."

"OK, we see the picture," interrupted Patricia. "He is trying to help. You don't make comments like that, normally."

"Sorry, I'm tired and, at the moment, it looks as though I'll either get arrested or killed before anyone can build a strong enough case. Are they going to inform us of progress?"

"The team will keep the colonel informed on orders from the commissioner."

"Miguel is not answering his phone," said Richard, still sounding grumpy.

"The detectives in Sheffield requested his return, so he is probably working on the train."

Patricia was doing her best to sound soothing, and he knew he was being unreasonable and ungrateful, but he couldn't help himself.

Julia returned to her office, asking that they keep her in the loop while he raided Patricia's drinks cabinet for a bottle of whisky and took it up to his room, leaving her to put the lunch things away. She had clients tomorrow and said she needed to prepare to be a therapist again. No one was happy with the situation. And so the day passed.

When he left the commissioner that morning, Miguel returned to his hotel and phoned both his team in Sarria and the general, his boss. The turn of events relieved both of them. He did his fair share of grovelling about the stupid mistakes he had made, and he wondered if this was the end of his career. Half an hour later, Sheffield called, asking him to come, so he had no time to dwell on it. When he went to catch a train, he intended to phone Patricia and Richard.

The last-minute ticket did not include a reserved seat, so he stood in the corridor with a family whose luggage and pushchair wouldn't allow them to look for seats, and entertained two toddlers to the obvious relief of their mother.

He wondered if he should have driven. He didn't remember Britain being so crowded when he had lived here or recall the crowded trains or the busy roads, but children see things differently. The toddlers here might

224

remember they had fun, not the lack of seats.

A young detective constable picked him up from the station, obviously in awe of him, standing to attention and calling him sir more often than he was used to. Once he arrived, the team was in full swing. So he never made his phone call.

The chief inspector ushered him to his office and asked about Jack.

"He was one of yours?" The DCI nodded.

"We've never lost a man before. It'll take time for the department to recover."

"What reports had you had from him prior to death?"

The Detective opened the door and shouted.

"Harrison." A dark-haired woman turned toward him.

"Have you got officer Dawson/ Clarke's reporting file handy?"

She stood up and grinned. "I'll get it." She reappeared two minutes later with a card folio.

"Are you Colonel López? Were you there when they discovered him? Poor Jack, it devastated us when we found out. He died a week before we heard anything."

Her boss was glaring at her. "That's enough, Jeani."

"I am acquainted with Jane Landis, and I am sorry about the delay. It took a while to get his ID confirmed. They had removed his paper ID before they put him in the water."

"He didn't drown, then?" asked Chief Inspector Robson.

"No. I gather that the Met never sent you the file."

"No, they didn't." He looked at the officer for confirmation. Inspector Harrison was shaking her head.

"I apologise once again. It was thoughtless of me not to ensure that you had a copy, but if you permit it, I will contact my team and get you copies of everything we have concerning this case. You need them anyway to assist with the crimes committed on your soil. Our justice department is deciding whether to request extradition for his murder and that of Molly Hardcastle/Hambleton. Much depends on what you can charge them with here, of course."

The rest of that day was busy. People asked about Jack so often that he suggested briefing the entire unit in one place. This was the sentiment that was missing when Jane arrived in Spain. He should have picked it up because losing a team member devastates morale for a while. He had misread her coldness as the professional front officers adopt when dealing with a body. But he should have realised finding a colleague breaks through that.

Someone booked him a hotel and the chief superintendent took him out to dinner, albeit a working one, thanking him for his help and hoping that the outcome suited both of them. He had no time for regrets or worry for his career.

They met in the dining room, a pleasant, discrete place decorated in muted colours and separated into areas with pot plants and screens.

"They, the commissioner's office, have asked us not to communicate with DCI Landis either to request anything or to give her information if she requests it. Should I infer they have contacted internal affairs?"

Miguel considered the senior police woman. She was as tall as he was, her hair, once blond streaked with silver grey, immaculately bobbed. But it was her eyes that he noticed, silver grey, matching her hair, and she looked directly at him. The frankness unnerved him and made it impossible to evade the question.

He wanted to show how important it was that no one spoke, but still avoid gossip.

"I have spoken with the commissioner about some worrying aspects of this case."

The chief superintendent was an intelligent woman.

"I see."

And her tone suggested that she understood, and the news didn't surprise her.

"We need a stroke of luck before someone else gets killed."

When she laughed, her face changed.

"In Sheffield, we call that good policing."

The phone woke Miguel up at four. Two men had broken into Tom Miller's house.

"Have you identified them?" he asked.

"Yes, their names only because they are refusing to speak. It's the same pair who appear on the cctv footage."

It may be an example of good policing, but the commissioner's efforts and a high-ranking Spanish guardia chief focused everyone's minds. Every officer on duty was alert and when the break-in happened. Control had dispatched a patrol car before Tom ended the call and the officers arrived as the intruders smashed the back door. The culprits were in cells an hour later when Miguel reached the office dealing with the incident.

The officer stood up and saluted when he entered.

"Ignore me. Let's get this incident closed. If you have a spare desk, I can keep out of everyone's way."

As he sat in the chair offered, he wondered if Richard's approach had rubbed off on him. Even a week earlier, he might have taken control of the briefing.

They identified the men as Simon Bassett and Mike Edgeware. They belonged to a group called One Nation, and both were on the police watch list for vandalism.

Tom had singled out Mike as part of the couple who

befriended them on the Camino, and they sent a team to his house to bring in his spouse.

Mike's partner admitted she travelled with him to Spain, and that Molly suggested it. They hadn't wanted Tom and Sally to know that they were meeting with groups of Spanish Nationalists to plan a co-ordinated attack on European cities. His wife stopped communicating then, realising that she had said too much. It was only when the group disowned them, leaving them to take the rap for four murders, that they started talking.

By 7 am, her solicitor arrived, and the interview continued.

"Give your version of the events that led to Molly's death first," suggested the Inspector.

"Someone tipped Micheal off the boyfriend might be a police officer."

"Who is Michael?"

" Michael Boolson, our leader."

"Are there any other leaders?"

"Yes Geraldine Brown, she was with us but travelling separately because of Tom, Sally and Jack. A Lord sponsors the groups. I have never met him, but he paid for our trip."

"So, can you confirm that Lord Bonham was the director of the group?"

"No, I know that someone with money pays for our journeys. I don't know the name. I only talk to Michael or Geraldine."

"So why did you kill Molly?"

She looked at her brief, who nodded.

"I didn't know she was dead until we got back. Molly and Jack were in love. He was a policeman, so I told Geraldine. I was expecting them to abort the mission."

"So the leader is Michael Boolson. Geraldine and

Michael coordinated everything, so they made all the decisions, for example. Was it Geraldine who commissioned Sally's murder and Tom's break-in?"

"I am not on the leadership team. I don't know who decides, but I always got the impression that both Geraldine and Michael sometimes followed orders from someone more important. There are other groups like ours. I learnt because we sometimes do things together. Maybe one person co-ordinates everything."

"And you have never been curious?"

"I enjoy the days out, but I don't want to organise them."

Mike gave them more information in his interview.

"Another member discovered Molly might become a traitor after overhearing a conversation between her and Jack before the walk started. By the time the news reached headquarters, we were halfway through the walk."

"Did you inform your wife of that?"

"No, nor did Geraldine. Molly and J were very close friends, so I was worried that she would warn her before we received further instructions."

"So it was Geraldine who suggested the Camino as cover for a planned exercise?"

"Oh no, the entire journey was genuine: Tom, Sally, and Molly talked about it for years before they set off. Geraldine saw it as an opportunity. She proposed we meet up with prominent Spanish nationalists at various places in the north of Spain."

"The journey changed Molly. She claimed she noticed God's presence or something," said Mike.

Then he asked for a coffee. "I have been up through the night."

"Yeah, breaking into someone's house. Do you want a reward for that?"

"My client is cooperating fully. If he gets a rest, that will continue. Would you like me to tell him to stop talking, or do you prefer to catch the real criminals here?"

"Thirty minutes, a drink, a sandwich and a bathroom break, and don't even think of asking for anything else or I'll charge your client under the terrorism act and send him to a dark hole where he might never see daylight again. The only reason that hasn't happened already is because he agreed to tell me what he knows."

The lawyer studied Miguel in disbelief.

"You don't want to know what happens to terrorists who threaten our national security," said the colonel.

An hour later, they were back. Mike was pale.

"We're not terrorists and it's a bit of graffiti, or stones thrown in protest, that's all."

"So you weren't planning to bomb the Cathedral?"

He went even paler. "No, I've explained. We were going to paint on the walls and hold up banners all harmless fun, which gets our point across to people."

The inspector shuffled his papers. "Did you attend any of the meetings?"

"No, that was Molly and Geraldine, while we kept the others distracted."

"Go on, let's hear the rest."

"Molly told my wife that she loved Jack, and we both realised that she was on the brink of giving it all up. She knew all the names of the group members and who planned every activity. We didn't kill her and her death surprised us."

Miguel lost his earlier control and banged on the table.

"What the bloody hell did you think would happen,

you idiot, that they would congratulate her on finding God and falling for a policeman? Did you imagine they would wish her good luck in her future life? What a bloody buffoon! You are the direct cause of three murders, and you still consider it harmless. Get out of my sight while I consider what else to charge you with. Sadly, stupidity is not illegal."

"Colonel…"

Miguel swung round and glared at the solicitor, who closed her mouth.

Then marched into the main office.

"I could use a coffee. That man has a public school education and a degree. What is the world coming to?"

"No argument from me, them kind of schools are a hotbed of som'att. The posh folk have every opportunity handed to them and waste it making trouble for those with nowt. Oh yes, he deserves what we can throw at him. Sir."

"Lets talk to his friend, shall we, and see what he does for fun."

Simon liked to brag and described with pride the activities involving the group, including Molly. Attacks on mosques, synagogues or people of colour in prominent positions. Social media posts to incite hatred. He didn't mind talking because he imagined he would be a hero in prison.

As he was a stereotypical skinhead, he looked dangerous. They must have included him because of his muscle, not because of his wits. He thought relieving wheelchair users of their wheelchairs and leaving them stranded was not only a fun Sunday afternoon pass-time, but was a contribution to British society.

Because he was proud of what he did, he provided a list of his bully boy friends and gave details of their activities, not realising he might go to Gaol for longer than those responsible.

Nothing led back to Lord Bonham because he made sure the trail of evidence stopped with Geraldine. For Miguel, that was a problem.

They brought in her for questioning soon after the arrest of Simon and Mike. The Chief Inspector was certain that she would either leave the country or go into hiding. She was packing when they arrived and Lord Bonham had disappeared. No one knew where he was.

# CHAPTER THIRTY-ONE

## *In the dark*

That day in London.

Richard was restless. He was concerned about the pressure he had put on Patricia and unsure how much he could trust Julia to save him, so his sleep that night was fitful and disturbed.

He woke early but, Patricia had told him she was going to the hospital early, so he took his time dressing after he had phoned John to ask if they needed help with compiling evidence. As he was getting ready, the doorbell rang, so he peeked through the window in case it was for him. Two plain clothed detectives and an unmarked car were there. His heart sank because he hadn't been able to reach Miguel and he didn't know at what stage the investigation was. As a precaution, he phoned Julia to ask her to meet him at the station, but voice-mail kicked in, so he left a message.

In the distance, he heard Mrs B answer the door, and the police ask for him, so he went downstairs, still putting on his jacket.

"I'm on my way, Mrs B. Don't worry," he called.

"Patricia says to use the upstairs sitting room," she said, as she disappeared to the basement.

As soon as she disappeared, the men pushed him through the open doorway, causing him to stumble and drop his stick. But they were ready for that and manhandled him toward the car. The shock kept him silent at first, and when he protested, they pushed him into the automobile and locked the door. One man sat beside him with the other in the driving seat.

"Be quiet and enjoy the ride," said the driver.

He prepared himself for the arrest, and the words scared him. The men were quiet, the atmosphere thick with their silence. His heart beat grew heavy and the effort of breathing took concentration.

"Where are we going?"

He slowly forced the words through dry lips.

They drove out of the city and ignored him. After two hours and with central London behind them, they stopped at a service station and handcuffed him to the door handle. A bathroom visit for them, leaving him unable to move. When they returned, they both got into the front seat. One of them set the GPS as if they hadn't known their destination before this.

The smaller of the two looked nervous, and the mood had changed.

"You told me that someone was meeting us here, and we just handed him over, saying that he had resisted arrest."

"Change of plan."

" Where are we heading? This is wrong and I don't like it. A bit of intimidation to please the boss doesn't hurt anyone, but this is plain wrong."

"We're off to Lord Bonham's house to leave him in an old chapel on the grounds. Someone else will pick him up later."

His hopes had risen when he realised that they didn't intend to kill him, but the new plan didn't sound good either. He strained to catch the conversation, but it stopped and an hour afterwards they drove into the estate, but turned off the drive at once into a small lane near the perimeter wall. The grounds were impressive and huge, and for fifteen minutes, they wound through trees toward a lake that he could see in the distance. They passed a couple of cottages, and sheep grazing between spaced oaks, and then into woodland, less well kept than the pasture, and turned off along a narrow, ill-maintained track.

"Are you sure this is it? It'll wreck the suspension."

"You put the coordinates in the gps."

The 'voice' told them they had reached their destination.

In front of them stood an ivy covered old chapel, in a poor state of repair with boarded windows. Weeds and brambles had taken over the gravel surrounding it. Further out, overgrown rhododendron bushes indicated formal planting had once existed here. His captors got out and walked off, leaving him to study his surroundings. Even overgrown, it was delightful, with the sun filtered by the rustling leaves, alive with birdsong. Gone were the sounds of urbanity prevalent in London. A bell tower in the small building added to the charm. Richard saw the remains of a formal garden stretching into the trees, amazed that his fear hadn't blinded him to the beauty of his location.

He assumed they'd come back for him after finding the

entrance. It was five long minutes later when they undid the handcuffs. They redid them as soon as they were out of the car, but stiff after sitting for three hours and with no stick, Richard stumbled, unable to walk.

Once again, they manhandled him, half-lifting and part-dragging because he was taller. Then shoved him through huge double doors, but not before one of them removed his phone. He fell, helpless to stop himself with his hands cuffed together, and hit the stone floor hard. He lay there, winded, for a while on the freezing flagstones. The damp stone was gritty and icy beneath his cheek, and he was angry with himself for not preventing this.

He stayed still until confident that moving was possible. In the meantime, the car started again, crunching along the gravel drive, so he knew he had been left alone. The temperature convinced him he needed to move, so he wriggled on his belly until he reached one of the shapes that loomed out of the darkness. A bench with a seat he could grab.

By pushing with his good leg, he moved into a sitting position, uncomfortable but an improvement on lying face to the floor. He had exhausted himself doing that much, but it was worth it.

It wasn't as gloomy as he first supposed. As his eyes adjusted to the light coming round the boarded windows, besides some furniture, he saw a door illuminated around the sides. Not having his hands free limited his movement, so he lacked anything to help him get there.

He had landed on his injured hip, and he was unsure if moving or resting was better. Panic was his enemy because the bleakness of his situation loaded his imagination with everything from rats to slow starvation, and not only that, the fear someone would come to finish him.

Why was he here was the biggest question? He had

expected to be in a police cell, but something had changed this morning.

By mid afternoon he had recovered enough to think about moving. The centre was empty, but with benches at the edges. A door in the corner was ajar, and he hoped it was a means of escape. He walked toward it but the pain kicked in and he stumbled, but even though every step took effort he preferred it to sliding along on his bottom, the other and more sensible possibility.

This was progress, despite expecting the main entrance to open at any moment and someone to come for him. Halfway there, he found a stick, a pole with the end broken off, the kind used for opening tall casements. Now he had a crutch and a weapon, not much but having it lifted his spirits.

The door, when he reached it, hid a surprise. There was light coming from a room at the top of a staircase. At the bottom was a Victorian restroom, unused for many years. He tried the tap, and to his amazement, water came out. It stuttered and groaned and was an alarming colour, but it worked, so he scooped a hand full into his mouth, gasping as it dripped on face and hands but too thirsty to care that the rusty brown hue hadn't cleared. Turning the tap off was harder, but after a protest, it moved.

The tiny window set deep into the wall was useless for escape, and that disappointed him. He hesitated, thinking that if he went upstairs, they might trap him with only a broken stick to defend himself, so he sat on the bottom step for a while, wondering what to do. Then realised his damaged leg meant he couldn't walk, let alone run. For him, it was safer to use his wits rather than escaping or defending himself. So he pulled himself up the steps, stopping several times to catch his breath, but he made it.

The room was square, and light flooded in through large windows on four sides. Furnished with a desk and chair, and a chaise longue, mouse eaten now, but still useful. A chest of drawers and a small fireplace completed the furnishings. Above each rectangular pane was another semi-circular stained glass picture window, which set the wooden floor alight with sunbeams. Rainbows emerged and then fragmented through the coloured panes.

This high up, he could see if anyone approached, even though branches of an adjacent tree blocked part of the view. The lane, a lawn and beyond that an unobstructed vista to the lake lay before him.

He pondered on breaking a window and jumping, but the ground fell away in front of the building, making the drop too great. Then he sank onto the chaise longue, intending to keep watch for a potential attacker, but woke up hours later, shivering and in need of the bathroom.

'So much for keeping watch,' he thought as he struggled to a sitting position hampered by the handcuffs.

The stairs were steep, and he was more afraid of descending that he had been of climbing them. Although he was slow, he made it without incident.

The tap opened more easily today and after a few minutes, the water ran clean and so he flushed the toilet, realising how lucky he was to have this. In fact, having slept for a couple of hours, he was feeling cheerful. Things could have been so much worse.

On reflection, his prison reminded him more of a Victorian folly than a church, the semi-usable spaces that were built to look impressive in the landscape, or be alone, or to meet a lover.

The building didn't appear to be utilised, but he hoped a previous visitor had left something helpful.

With the last of the light for illumination, he felt his way using the stick to check for obstacles in the shadows, passing two wooden benches before reaching the front. There he found a table with a drawer containing candles, matches and a cigarette lighter, a satisfactory haul if difficult to carry.

The next step was to try to light the candle, so he tried the lighter, but it was useless. The matches provided him with hope and when the very first match produced a flame, he couldn't believe his luck, and his view improved. A chest of drawers behind the table yielded a candlestick, a cup and saucer, and a moth-eaten tablecloth. Now to carry them back. It took him several attempts to move with his light intact to return.

That done, he retired to his eyrie and set the taper on the candlestick. Dusk fell, and no one arrived and maybe no one knew his location other than the men who left him. It was dark outside now, and he was glad of the flickering flame because it meant he could explore the Desk. There was a dried up ink bottle and a broken quill pen, a pile of shredded paper, the result of mice, and nothing else.

The chest of drawers was better, a blanket albeit with holes, mice again, he suspected, two more candles, a board game and playing cards.

The bottom drawer fell apart when he pulled it, but was empty, so he wondered if the rest might break, and decided to try.

The desk, chair and chaise longue were heavy Victorian pieces, but the drawers were cheap pine and much later, carried here by kids wanting a den, he decided.

When he banged the shattered section hard onto the floor and it cracked enough for him to force it apart. So he had wood for fire, a candle, a broken cup of water, and he was alive. What more could he want? Everything he needed to spend the night relatively comfortably was here. If he slept, he hoped that by morning he'd have a clear head to form a plan.

When Richard woke up the next day, he was feeling neither fortunate nor happy. In fact, he was freezing, hungry, and anxious. The failure of someone to come was not the reprieve he expected. He might have cheated death, but with no means to escape, he risked hypothermia. Both his legs and the handcuffs hampered him, making climbing and jumping painful, and only as a very last resort.

He limped to the bathroom, washed in the freezing water, and took a drink. The exercise warmed him and helped him think.

By the time he got upstairs, he had a plan. First, breaking up the chest which, although flimsy, resisted his efforts. The drawers broke after much hard work, but the outside case refused to budge. He needed more firewood for his proposition to work.

He lit the fire with what he had. Another hour of endeavour, blowing on embers and fanning, gave fledgling flames, which at least kept his mind off his hunger and the increasing pain in his hip. Once he had a blaze. He found the evaporated ink and took it downstairs. Slowly again, he cursed himself, his leg, his plight, and then at last he prayed to have enough patience and determination to, at least, get his plan underway.

He half-filled the bottle with water and shook it. Bit by bit the powder dissolved, leaving the brilliant blue colour that reminded him so much of school. When he got upstairs, the sun was high in the sky and the temperature creeping higher. He fed the flames using most of his meagre pile of timber. Then ripped off a tiny strip of blanket and wrapped it around the broken pen, making a paintbrush of sorts, and started painting his message on the windows. HELP in big letters at the top part of each glass pane. He needed to stand on the chair and use the wooden sill to balance. It was exhausting, but he stopped only to tend the fire. He couldn't do anything after the third window. He gazed at the fine window pane, knowing that no amount of determination would get him there.

Warm and comfortable due to the flames and the sun, he lay on the chaise longue and drifted off to sleep. When he woke up, night was falling and there was banging downstairs. Friend or foe, he welcomed the sound and tried to sit up, but the pain forced him back. Every part of him was stiff and sore, but his leg and hip were painful beyond belief, any movement sending spikes of agony along his spine.

The thumping stopped and Richard realised he had assumed that someone had a key. He had heard the police officers lock the door behind them and, having used it, they must have taken it with them. So if anyone came, they needed a second one to enter. The panic started to churn his stomach.

He thought again of breaking a window with the last pieces of wood, but when he moved, the pain shot through his frame, forcing him back, energy spent. As he was too tired to climb, he closed his eyes, realising as he did that if he broke the glass, the temperature would fall.

He was too tired to cry or show emotion. The fire had burned to embers, but Richard couldn't break more wood. And he wondered if hypothermia hurt and he could sleep and not wake.

He was unsure how long he lay shrouded in misery and threatened by encroaching panic. He wished he had written a note thanking Patricia for her help and another to Miguel explaining what had happened. It would be possible if he woke up in the morning, but he wasn't sure if he wanted to wake up. The gloom paralysed and disabled him. Deceiving him that death was better than life. Then he prayed, but not for rescue. He was beyond believing that.

"Father in heaven, don't allow me to lose hope. Don't let the darkness take me."

Afterwards, he closed his eyes, and he knew that time was passing because the dusk outside was getting deeper.

Then, as faith faded, the banging came again, now accompanied by shouting and drilling. He reached for the stick, but he couldn't get even that far.

# CHAPTER THIRTY-TWO

*In the meantime.*

Miguel left another message on Richard's phone asking him to call. It worried him that his colleague was at the mercy of Chief Inspector Landis, for the moment at least. Alerting her might compromise the forthcoming inquiry. They needed their suspects to be in custody first.

Tiredness, a sense of failure, the worry over his friend, and frustration over collecting information contributed to his emotional state.

Tomorrow morning was the soonest the unit could get the evidence ready.

He lacked sleep, but the day continued to be busy interviewing Simon and Mike, and then they charged Mike's wife as an accessory to murder.

A team was by now searching Geraldine's apartment. She was at home packing a bag when they arrived. They were bringing her to Sheffield for an interview. Miguel had requested an extradition order because there was plenty of evidence to charge her with Molly's death. They needed luck or a confession to involve her with Jack's.

They were gathering material against the 'One Nation Group'. Once the links became plain, they interviewed them and they were implicating each other. The Sheffield anti-terror squad was having a field day rounding up culprits.

The organisation had 'elite' and activist members. It functioned by rewarding members for their 'loyalty' and punishing them for asking difficult questions.

The Westminster Exhibition recruited members with trained the staff to spot suitable candidates. Lord Bonham remained in charge from the shadows. He gained more and more power, buying shares in media companies, befriending and funding members of Parliament and funding lobbying groups.

His disappearance caused concern.

It was difficult locating members of the elite group too, and when they did, it was hard to link them with the most serious crimes.

It was mid-afternoon when Miguel tried his friend again, and then Patricia.

"I'm so glad that you've phoned. Richard is missing."

"What do you mean?"

"Two police officers came for him, so he left a message for Julia, but nobody at the station knows anything about it."

"I haven't been able to reach him on the phone."

"Nor can anyone."

"Did the detectives give their names?"

"No, but my housekeeper told me she would recognise them if she saw them again."

"And Jane Landis?"

"Has taken a few days' leave. Nobody can tell me her

location."

"She has learnt what's happening. Patricia, I'll come back to you. Try not to worry, keep trying to discover where Richard is. I need to speak to someone."

The commissioner listened and then suggested he start the corruption enquiry, sending a team into Jane's department at once. He promised resources were available to find Richard, but it took time to get them into place, although they alerted the internal investigation unit. When Miguel phoned back, Patricia told him she couldn't locate Richard. She had tried hospitals without success; he wasn't being kept in a police cell anywhere near London, and despite Julia's phone calls, no one admitted to knowing the officers who came to the house.

They were worried. If Jane Landis had heard the new direction that the investigation had taken, she may have fled much earlier than she intended, covering her tracks where possible. Then dumped Richard somewhere, to give her enough time to get away. They alerted public transport to lookout for her and the professor. There was no sign of either.

Miguel spoke to Inspector Davis and requested that he phone around private airports.

"I think I have located DCI Landis and Lord Bonham, sir," Davis said.

"Found them or established their trail?" Miguel asked.

"Yes, sorry, their trail. If it is them, they posted a flight plan to a small Croatian airport, leaving yesterday afternoon. The ground staff recognised Lord Bonham because he and the pilot have flown before. John has gone with photos to verify the identity and get the details.

"Did they have ID and passports?" asked Miguel.

"Their ID appeared valid. However, the names they

used are different. John will learn more when he arrives. I'll call as soon as I learn anything more."

Miguel remained busy for the rest of the day. They interviewed Geraldine, but the interview stalled when she called for a counsellor and again because Lord Bonham's lawyer, who she requested, refused to represent her. In the end, Sir Giles sent his solicitor along, but only after a heated conversation with the chief inspector. Sir Giles not only didn't believe that his assistant had committed any of the crimes, but insisted he couldn't manage without her and it was imperative that they released her.

Geraldine said little at first, denying everything. However, as soon as she realised that the Professor/ Lord Bonham had left her to take the blame, she became rattled. Miguel was certain that she would talk, so they charged her and took her to the cells.

The Colonel then phoned Davis to see what had happened with their information collection. He reported progress, as they had completed the important parts and were nailing the finer details. Others offered evidence now that the commissioner was involved, and they had enough to convict Jane Landis.

When he retired, Richard was still missing, so he planned to take the train to London the following morning.

Miguel caught the early commuter line after he had checked with Patricia. He booked a ticket in first-class, knowing that it was full, and he needed to spend the time working. He got the last seat and paid a small fortune for it.

Where had they taken Richard? The intention must have been to arrest him using planted or falsified evidence. Since Jane Landis only wanted to discredit him and not convict him, it was straightforward. By then, they had done enough damage.

Miguel went straight to Patricia's house, eager to offer his support in the search for Richard. When he arrived, her distress was obvious. She had made phone calls to hospitals and the police in different places, with frustrating results because he was an adult resident in Spain. He wasn't missing. They would contact the Spanish law enforcement to determine if he had reached home, but no more. If he had gone back to Spain to avoid arrest, they would follow the proper procedures.

Another case kept Julia in her office this morning, so when he arrived, Patricia was alone and pleased to receive him. The wait is harder than taking action, even if the action changes nothing or makes things worse.

Miguel, without thinking, took charge, suggesting coffee and pen and paper.

"Let's use a logical approach, choosing the most likely scenarios which we will rule out one by one."

"I have tried the hospitals and police stations."

"I think the detectives were there to arrest him, but they aborted the plan when Jane Landis realised she needed to leave and make Richard disappear until she had escaped."

"Do you know where she is?" Patricia asked.

"Yes, they used a private plane to escape the country."

"Lord Bonham, doesn't he have a large country estate somewhere?"

"Does he?" Miguel became interested.

"It's the perfect place to hide someone."

"Absolutely. It will be difficult getting permission to search, though."

"Don't worry, there is a way. You realise Richard might not..."

"Stop there!" said Patricia. "Without hope, we have nothing. Let's be positive till we have reason to change our minds."

"OK."

The policeman thought his colleague was dead, but still wanted someone searching for him.

Time was short, and they needed him.

In the meantime, he asked her to research Lord Bonham's estate. She was an extra pair of hands and it saved time.

Miguel headed for the office of administration and statistics.

Chief Superintendent Bolin was a small fussy man with an empty desk and no visible furniture on which to keep his paperwork.

The colonel was at his most charming, but he was getting impatient. The material that the team had been putting together fell into two categories. Evidence relating to the bombing and proof that Jane Landis had falsified the paperwork intended for the prosecution. And historical records of corruption by Lord Bonham and his group.

The quick thinking of Inspector Davis and his band of dissenters had saved much of what they demanded. They wanted to use it in the best way possible. The Sheffield police were still questioning Geraldine regarding the death of Richard's wife, and Miguel needed her statement for extradition.

Chief Superintendent Bolin wanted every loose end chased up before handing over the details. The colonel tried to persuade him that time was the biggest issue because of the possibility of the leadership escaping. In which case, those responsible wouldn't face prosecution, but their workers would. In Miguel's book, an unsatisfactory outcome. He had seen it before, but it always galled him. Prosecuting the foot soldiers never ended the war.

# CHAPTER THIRTY-THREE

*The suspects.*

Miguel ran across the platform to catch the Sheffield train on his way to question Geraldine again. The file, which was strong enough to get her remanded in custody, was in his bag. Extradition to Spain was a possibility, but he wanted to minimise the chance of her slipping between the cracks and leaving the country.

He got Richard listed as a missing person, and an alert sent out to the police, who dealt with the Bonham family estate. Not a search warrant, but progress none the less. He was not at his best, having missed breakfast and lunch. The train was not crowded, and to his delight, had a dining car, so he collected sandwiches and a drink.

The Spanish timetable is so different from the British one that he became disoriented when he was in Britain. People never stopped to enjoy a meal. He sat with his sandwiches, observing the mother and daughter in the two opposite seats. Their interaction caused him to miss his family, making him homesick.

He had become bogged down in this case, and he felt a failure. Even rushing to London was stupid when could have liaised with police from his hotel room and reassured Patricia with a phone call. Would he ever learn he was no longer an action man? He needed to work from a desk, trust his team, and change the way he dealt with cases. That takes time, and he hoped for the chance.

His mobile rang. It was Chus from his team.

"Piece of luck boss, we found Jack's mobile and all of his ID."

"How on earth...?"

"Seems a cyclist nipped for a pee in the woods, and there they were. He handed them in to the local police in Paradela."

"How come we only just got them?"

"Took a while to connect the dots. Best thing is a fingerprint."

"Geraldine!"

Miguel's mood changed, and he couldn't wait to be interviewing her.

By the time he arrived back, Sir Giles was there proclaiming that his personal assistant was innocent and the duty officer was trying to keep him calm. Miguel spoke to the sergeant, showing his ID.

"Might I suggest I speak to the minister? Perhaps you could tell Chief Inspector Robson and then arrange for an office for us to talk."

The policeman looked relieved. "There is a room. I'll just phone the DCI and tell him. Shall I get some coffee brought in, sir?"

"Thank you," he turned to Sir Giles. "Shall we?"

"The loyalty to your staff is commendable. However, there is evidence she committed several murders, including that of your daughter and her boyfriend, Jack."

"That's rubbish. Molly and Geraldine were friends. Does she still need a lawyer?"

He needed to convince the man to leave before he got upset.

"I sent my man up last night."

"It was the best gift you could give her because we need to question her again. The detective here will charge her if that hasn't happened, and we plan to ask the judge to remand her into custody."

Sir Giles looked shocked.

"But I have lost Molly."

" Yes, I know, and I'm sorry. Is there anyone to stay with you when you return home?"

The chief inspector arrived during the exchange.

"He's right, sir." He held out his hand and introduced himself. "Even if your personal assistant has done nothing wrong, it will take a few days to sort out, but there is evidence she needs to explain."

The politician looked defeated. "There is a driver waiting. Could you call me at my club if there is anything I can do?"

He handed a card to Inspector Robson, and they ushered him out.

"Is he involved, do you think?"

"Certainly she is more than a PA, but it's hard to conceive of his involvement."


Miguel was watching the interview with Geraldine as it was being filmed. Later, he planned to question her and explain how the European arrest warrant worked, hoping Brexit and the nature of this case didn't complicate the procedure.

She said little other than denying knowledge of conspiracy or organised crime. Although she admitted she was a friend of Lord Bonham, she didn't mention his politics. This continued until her solicitor demanded they either charge her or release her, as they were getting nowhere. The chief inspector agreed, and they ended the interview to bring in Miguel.

The colonel read the formal charges, adding that they now had conclusive proof that she had killed Jack Clark. Disclosure of the evidence took place over the next twenty-four hours, but explained the British police had their own warrant. Then he played out a hunch.

"At the moment, we are chasing Lord Bonham and Chief Inspector Landis, who are evading justice. They have a romantic relationship and escaped together." Geraldine had gone pale.

"No. That's not possible, Greg and Jane. No."

"Yes, they have left evidence that points at your orchestrating it all. In the end, if we can't find them and question them, we will charge you with each crime, including instigating all the 'One Nation's' group activities." Miguel stood up to show he planned to speak with the solicitor once they had brought the charges.

When he left, they produced more offences before taking Geraldine to the cells to await a hearing.

Most solicitors had never dealt with a European arrest warrant, so Miguel, because it made court cases smoother, handed him an information pack outlining who to contact and where to find them.

An hour later, he was sitting in the superintendent's office, discussing what happened next.

"This has become a very high profile case, and the chief constable wants a personal report. Do we have everything tied down?"

"If we had Gregory Bonham and Jane Landis in custody, we would feel better. We know they arrived in Croatia and left again for Belarus."

"I'm certain they then went further afield. I have contacts in Belarus who can confirm they landed, but from experience we will have a hell of a job getting any official information. At a guess, they plan to change identities there, having transferred money."

"Geraldine is going to answer to the offences, even though someone else paid her.

There may be a discussion on where she serves her sentence."

"That decision is political, I'm sure."

"Oh, I don't know. I consider she might trade information on Bonham and Landis for some consideration of the sentence and may plead guilty to some charges."

"I don't think so. She is a paid assassin They chose her for her hardness. She is a psychopath."

Miguel grinned. "An assassin in love with a psychopath."

"To murder so many, you must lack emotion," said the chief inspector.

"Love is diverse. Now the Duke has betrayed her, she will try to gain back some control over her situation."

# CHAPTER THIRTY-FOUR

*And at last*

*Meanwhile, on Lord Bonham's estate.*

After a while, Richard was aware of his name being called and shouted. There was bumping and shouting downstairs, but despite his best efforts, he could not move his leg. The door opened and a powerful torch shone in his eyes, blinding him. A uniformed police officer was holding the torch, and he lowered it.

"Would you be Mr Harris, sir?" Richard's uncertainty silenced him.

He tried to focus on the uniform but it didn't stay still and before he could reply, Patricia pushed past into the room.

"It is, and we need an ambulance."

"I would prefer fish and chips," said Richard at last.

He didn't move, despite the mixture of relief, embarrassment, and pain.

"How on earth did you find me?"

"An estate worker saw smoke, and checked. They've had problems with tramps before. When he arrived and the door was locked and the key missing and your message was on the window so he rang the police. The office had already received the message to search for you, sir," said the young PC.

"Can you stand up, or even move?" His friend asked.

Patricia put her hands on her hips, reminding him of the first day they met. He had been collecting Gill from the house they shared when Patricia had looked at him, taking the same stance.

"You don't appear to be her type."

Nervous, he hadn't known what to do, so he had kept quiet.

"Well, do you speak?" she had said.

He laughed at the memory and Patricia, whose telepathic powers were remarkable, laughed with him.

You haven't changed, you still have nothing to say.

"I seem to have damaged my hip again."

Then she turned to the constable.

"Officer, I'm pretty certain that was an understatement, so we'll need a stretcher if you could tell the paramedics when they arrive?"

They were only alone for a minute before a sergeant arrived.

"Are you up to answering some questions, sir?"

After confirming Richard's identity, the policeman explained that DCI Lovegrove planned to come and see him in the hospital.

"Today, I'll be asking basic questions, sir. I understand there were comments made in parliament and the commissioner has become involved. So taking your statement is above my pay grade." Richard detected disappointment in the sergeant's voice.

"Are you able to describe the two men, sir?"

"I can do better if you give me a pencil and paper. I'll draw sketches of them for you."

"That would be helpful."

"Do you remember anything about the car?"

He made this sergeant's day.

"A blue Nissan reg number*******."

"Sergeant, I believe the men were only acting on the orders of Chief Inspector Landis."

He closed his eyes and wished the world was gone. That he was on his back, dirty and in agony, and the faces etched sympathy regarded him with communal pity emphasised his helplessness.

"Yes, sir, all the same. It's not right."

At that moment, his radio made a loud static noise.

"Excuse me, sir."

He moved to stand by the window, to get better reception. "That's someone arrived to remove those cuffs for you. Sorry about the delay, sir."

The observation surprised Richard. The young constable must have noticed the handcuffs earlier, then asked for a locksmith when he radioed for an ambulance.

Patricia's alarmed expression when she noticed them stuck in his mind for a long time afterwards.

"Handcuffs. Oh my God, what next?"

He could hear voices further away and the room filled with people.

A needle prick was followed by a lessening of the pain and when the paramedics loaded him onto the gurney and put him on a drip to examine his leg, he almost passed out. But soon they had him stabilised with an inflatable splint and on his way and Patricia went with him.

"Did Gill cope with this level of excitement for twenty years?"

" Twenty-five."

"It's worse than I thought."

Today he appreciated Patricia's conversation because it kept the focus away from him. Moving him had triggered the pain, and he wanted to scream, but he took a deep breath and tried smiling in response, but didn't know if he succeeded.

*Several weeks later.*

Richard regarded Patricia with suspicion.

" No, no, no, I don't require a therapist, no matter how qualified."

"Of course it is your choice."

"But, there is a but in your statement," he didn't hide his annoyance.

"Look, you need a wheelchair because it enables you, as a tool, to protect your independence. In the same way, a therapist will give you the tools to keep your thoughts independent. Remember, a traumatised mind needs help."

Her voice was low, and she spoke with patience. He hunched in the bed, his fists balled under the covers, fighting his emotions because she was right.

Miguel arrived at that moment, dispersing the tension.

"I'm here for two days clearing up loose ends and to bring some good news."

Then he put a pile of books on Richard's table.

"About the case?"

Richard was eager to keep the conversation away from himself.

"Geraldine has given us a lot of information about

Gregory Bonham, everything from how he transfers his finances to where he will travel to and a list of other associates and their involvement.

Of course, in exchange for considerations in her own trial."

"So everyone is happy?" asked Patricia.

"No, we are not there yet."

With so much experience, Miguel was immune to happily ever after stories.

"Here is your passport."

In the way of magicians, he pulled it out of his pocket with a flourish.

"Does that mean I'm no longer a suspect?"

"Two young detective constables have admitted to tampering with evidence, so you will get an official apology and some compensation."

"That's something I suppose."

"Are you coming back to Spain?"

Richard looked puzzled. "That's where my home is."

"After all this… I just wondered…"

"I need Galicia more than ever but the trouble is, my house isn't wheelchair accessible and I'm not sure that I can use my shower."

"When will you be fit to travel?"

"Flying and the danger of blood clots is the problem. I would like to rehab in Spain, so would my insurance company, but I require help and I can't afford to pay a nurse."

"Is that not covered by insurance?" She was used to it being free in the health service.

Richard leaned back.

"Flying is, but I'm not allowed because of the danger of aneurysm. My energy won't deal with all the clauses."

Patricia looked thoughtful. "Can I ask Julia to look into it?"

Richard's eyelids were drooping, so he nodded towards his bedside table where the documents were. She searched inside, but he had closed his eyes and was falling asleep. He heard them slip out, but nothing after that.

*Six months later, in Galicia.*

Miguel stood. "Shall I get you another beer, Richard?"

They were sitting in Miguel's garden with Carolina and the children, who were running in circles round the pergola. They needed shade due to the hot weather, and it was a very pleasant way to enjoy a Sunday afternoon. Miguel handed out the beers.

"If you are here permanently, will it be logistically complicated?"

"I have an entire department to organise, not just an operational team. I can run everything from my Sarria office. It means I'm more or less desk-bound and Manuel takes charge of the current operational unit. I was reluctant to give up the good stuff, so I interfered. Now I'm recruiting teams. If you join us, you'll be part of the first. Sarria has had a major technology upgrade, creating job opportunities, so it is favourable for the town."

"Also convenient for the family," added Carolina.

"Will you be able to stay desk-bound?"

"After the balls up I made of the Molly Hardcastle case, my squad plan to handcuff me to my chair if I impede operations." Everyone laughed now.

"Did you discover why Geraldine killed her outside Richard's house?" asked Caroline.

" Yes, it was because she had fallen in love with Jack and was planning to end the criminal activity she may not have succeeded because people don't change their politics. She said she would confess to her part in the bombing and blame Geraldine for Gill's death. Molly had tried to get your wife to leave, and she had refused, so she threatened her with an antique knife, but Gill slipped and she got stabbed. However, she would be alive if Geraldine had not arrived and ushered everyone away, including the security and ambulance staff. Gill had seen too much and Geraldine was afraid she would talk. Some of that is guesswork and we will never know whether she killed Molly in cold blood."

At the trial, she said this.

"Molly said an ex-police officer lived on the Camino. She was going to report everything. When she discovered it was chief inspector Harris, she wanted to express sorrow about her part in his wife's death, even if it meant prison. The policeman must have lost his temper and killed her. "

"Wow! I'm lucky then!"

"Not when the court heard details of your alibi. No, they were unanimous in finding her guilty of Molly's murder."

"But the judiciary allowed her to plead guilty to the manslaughter of Gill?"

"Our job is to catch them," said Miguel, with a sigh. "Then the politicians take over." He made such a funny face that the serious mood evaporated.

"How is your house?" asked Carolina, changing the subject.

"I love it, and your friend Marcos produced an amazing design. I expected it to look like the disabled toilet in a motorway services, but I was wrong."

He had struggled with his recovery and his now visible disability and even after he had taken Patricia's advice and gone to therapy, he noticed concern in the eyes of his friends.

"There are still bad days, but it helps to live somewhere so beautiful. Having such good friends makes the biggest difference."

"The pilgrim painting is in the dining room because I have seen nothing that captures the dawn with so much finesse. Are you sure you want us to have it?"

"I hope it reminds you that every day is new. Besides, every time I touch it, someone gets killed." There was an entire minute's silence before they started laughing.

# THANK YOU FOR READING MY BOOK.

Thank you for reading my book.

If you enjoyed this novel, please leave a review on Amazon or Goodreads

Please visit my website, Abigail Thorne Author.

https://abigailthorneauthor.WordPress.com/

If you want to ask me a question

or have spotted a dastardly mistake which needs eradicating forthwith.

Email me direct at.

Abigailthorne1@outlook.com

# AKNOLWLEDGMENTS

There are many people needed to get a book to publication stage. Without the following wise souls, I would never have succeeded. I cannot thank them enough.

Steve, my ever patient husband.

My Friends and fellow authors Galicia.

Printed in Great Britain
by Amazon